THE PLACE OF BELONGING

A MEMOIR

Jayne Pearson Faulkner

Carmichael
PUBLISHING
A DIVISION OF DEEP RIVER BOOKS

The Place of Belonging

Published by
Carmichael Publishing
Sisters, Oregon
http://www.carmichaelpublishing.com

ISBN-10 1-935265-45-8
ISBN-13 978-1-935265-45-0

Library of Congress Control Number: 2010941289

Printed in the USA

Cover and interior design by Robin Black, www.blackbirdcreative.biz

Dedicated to Grandma
Maude Davis Olson
for her sacrifice, love, and care.

First and foremost to Nancie and Bill Carmichael, editors and publishers extraordinaire. Your input and advice is superb, and your encouragement awesome. And to all my other siblings, as well as my husband, children, grandkids, nieces and nephews who thought my small story worthwhile, because it was, and is, for them.

CONTENTS

There are places we all come from—
Deep-rooty-common places—that make us who we are.
And we disdain them or treat them lightly at our peril.
We turn our backs on them at the risk of self-contempt.
There is a sense in which we need to go home again—
And can go home again.
Not to recover home, no. But to sanctify memory.

—ROBERT FULGHUM[1]

1 Robert Fulghum, *From Beginning to End: The Rituals of Our Lives* (New York: Villard Books, 1995), 200

CHAPTER ONE

BIG SKY PEOPLE

I WAS BORN IN THE BIG SKY COUNTRY—sky that was tacked from one edge of the prairie to the other in a billowing tent of blue. It was always blue.

I heard the song, "Ole Buttermilk Sky," on the little table-top radio and ran outside to stare up at the sky, wondering what buttermilk had to do with it. Buttermilk was what my mother liked to drink, cold in a plain tall glass. I tasted it once and spit it out. The sky was not like that. Every day its sweet blueness stretched away to forever.

My world under this big sky was cramped, though, and restricted to a few blocks north and south of the tiny rented house on the alley where I lived. My grandmother saw to that: my grandmother, whose strict dark eyes held secrets of pain seldom spoken.

In this city-town of Great Falls, Montana, my world extended a block south to where my best friend Willow lived in an apartment. I was allowed to go that far on my roller skates over the split and cracked sidewalk. It also extended a few blocks north to my school where I walked every day and learned about when the explorers had drawn near the Great Falls with breathless souls while the Indians still possessed the wind-clawed plains.

Two blocks farther north was our church, a white clapboard affair with tacked-on steps and across the way from an elegant stone church that looked like a fortress. I thought it had probably been there since before the Indians. I had gone to that stone church with Grandma to a banquet one night. She told me to wear my best dress. And I was told to sit up nicely at a long table with a paper tablecloth and not run around and play like my friend Wally was doing. "No running," she said. "That's not for you! Just eat and mind your manners." Still, churches with food were more fun than just sitting quietly on pews and listening. But my mother and grandmother liked the little white church better, so that was where we walked—every Sunday.

Sometimes I rode on the city bus with my grandmother to where the downtown lay in long gray rows of stores, saloons, and a movie theater. Great Falls was busier now than it used to be. Things were stirring and a war was going on in far-off places across the ocean. A war with Germany and now one with Japan, and Great Falls had a military base. Air Force men in uniform and young girls with bright red lipstick and upswept hair swirled around these streets. I liked to look at them and wonder if my daddy was perhaps an Air Force man, tall and handsome in his uniform.

He was, but I didn't know it then. Years later I found out he had left town and joined the Air Force the day he got the message to meet my mother at the Top Notch Café. She had something to tell him. He didn't even wait to find out what it was. So my world was my mother, my grandmother, and my little space in Great Falls, securely enclosed by my grandmother's strong, sunburned arms of protection.

I sometimes wished I were pretty like my mother, whose shiny auburn hair was always pulled back and carefully styled around her face. But I wasn't pretty like that. My hair was brown, and I had a dimple in my chin that my mother didn't have. Grandma didn't even have it.

"So where did I get it?" I remember asking Grandma a long time ago.

She dug around in her box of pictures, pulled out an old photo of a young girl with dark hair and eyes and a cleft chin, clearly visible in the picture. "Your aunt Ruby," Grandma said. "My oldest daughter. Died when she was only twenty-two, life just getting started." Grandma had sighed, and I knew not to ask her more, lest I uncover the tender wound still hidden there.

My mother Harriet went to work every day in a beauty salon on Central Avenue. Sometimes on Saturdays, I went there, too. I'd watch the row of ladies sitting under machines that looked like they could kill. Long wires with metal clips snaked from under the hoods and clamped onto their heads. But the ladies seemed to like it. They were all smiling and reading magazines.

I wondered what I would do when I grew up and decided this was it. When I told my mother, she shook her head and said, "*No.* You'll be a teacher, because they don't have to stand up all day long and get varicose veins. Or better yet," her voice softened, "a *missionary.* You can be a missionary."

I hadn't known my mother when she liked to go to parties and dance the night away. Grandma told me about that. After I was born, Harriet had found the Lord. *Found the Lord* was what Grandma said. "Just what I prayed for," Grandma told me.

I could see sometimes—like now, when my mother was looking across the room like it wasn't there—that she wanted more in life than the Doll House Beauty Salon. Something more. But I liked my life now. I still wanted to be a beautician, but I decided not to mention it to her again.

Some of my mother's best clients were Air Force officers' wives. I saw them when I would visit the shop with Grandma on a Saturday afternoon. They smelled like the kind of perfume that came in a blue bottle. Mom had some—it was called "Evening in Paris." They smelled like that. Some had strange accents, a deep soft way of talking and saying "y'all," like they didn't belong in Montana. My mother would pile their hair in long rolls up the sides, or sweep it up from their faces into a bundle of curls on top.

There was only one client she would not accommodate: the Lieutenant Major's wife. She had come in one afternoon, insisting on a perm, though it had not been scheduled. My mother had told us all about it when she got home. I was sick that day and my high fever was not responding to Grandma's Vicks VapoRub remedy. So Mom was leaving early, when the Lieutenant Major's wife swirled in.

"I've got a party tomorrow night, and I need a permanent wave," she announced. "This is the only day all week I can do it. What with three other parties coming up—"

"Oh, I'm sorry," my mother said. "You don't have an appointment, and I'm leaving early. My little girl is sick." Mom searched for a softening of the other woman's brittle and demanding face. She just stared at Mom and drew on her long cigarette. The air clouded with smoke.

"I'm sorry," Mom said again. She pointed to an empty perch in a booth and continued, "But Amy over there had a cancellation, and she has time."

More smoke curled out through the scarlet lips. "I do not go to Amy."

"Well, I'm sorry." Mom took her sweater off the hook by the door.

The woman pounded her cigarette out on the tin ashtray shaped like the state of Montana. "You know, I could ruin your business here by a single word."

"My little girl is sick," my mother repeated as she closed the door behind her. She breathed in the fall air, all clean and shivery—just like she felt inside. Amy would give the lady a perm, but if she never came back and made good on her threat, so be it.

This all contrived to make her somehow mysterious, this hairdresser who had turned away the Lieutenant Major's wife. It was on record that she would not do her hair again. From then on, it was hard to get an appointment in the Doll House Salon with the slim, auburn-haired one named Harriet. You had to call weeks in advance.

And then one brightly-shining Sunday when the the ugly, slush-filled alley had turned a dirty gray—she met him at church. The little white church, with the same old people, all at once sported Someone New. Said he was only visiting, had to spend the night in Great Falls, but never missed church.

I didn't see him at all. I was busy talking to my friend Nedra about when I could play at her house, wondering if Grandma would ever let me. But Mom told me about their first meeting later—over and over, whenever I begged her.

There he was: shy, handsome, and steely-blue eyed, like his Scandinavian ancestors had looked before him as they stepped off a Viking ship to discover Greenland. He noticed my mother's auburn hair first, as it caught a gleam of light from the oval-shaped window.

And she had seen him, had noticed how his neatly combed thin brown hair needed a slight trim. And those eyes. They were so blue, almost cold blue, like an ice-fed mountain lake.

My grandmother and I left church shortly after the service was over, quickly walking home to fix dinner. Mom lingered to visit with friends, trying not to look at the stranger, who was trying not to look at her. And when they were the only two left in the little white church, they said hello, how are you, and what is your name.

He was a farmer, he said, and my mother glanced down at his big, wind-chapped hands. He farmed with his three brothers and a sister, up north of Great Falls, about sixty miles. North of the little town of Conrad. It was pretty nice, he said, especially in spring.

My mother's small, well-manicured hand grasped her black Bible and held it to her chest. "It was nice meeting you," she said. "Hope you can come back again." She was breathing too hard, but he didn't notice, just stepped to his little black Plymouth and drove away.

CHAPTER TWO

GUNDER

GRANDMA HAD MADE AN EXTRA BAKED POTATO, just in case. But my mother didn't seem to notice—or at least made no mention of it—as she slipped in, closed the door behind her and sat quietly at the table while we ate.

My grandmother brought up the subject of the new man at church as she was clearing the table. I said right out loud that I hadn't noticed any stranger at all. "Just as well," Grandma said. "Best to keep away from strangers anyway—even those that go to church."

"His name's Gunder Pearson," Mom said. "He's a Swede."

Grandma nodded. "Like your father." She reached in the dishpan for the pot scrubber. The rest she said to herself: *They're quiet; they're stubborn; and they get sick. Leave you all alone in this world with kids to raise.*

"We'll never see him again anyway," my mother said, ending the conversation. And our lives went on as before—our lives on a cold Sunday afternoon, when the sun was shining.

He was at prayer meeting two weeks later. Had trouble with the Plymouth, he told Mom, and had to bring it back to the dealership. He stayed on since it was church night, and he couldn't miss prayer meeting, he said.

My mother didn't like to miss prayer meeting, either, but she sometimes did. Now she had been there two weeks in a row, her legs aching from her day's work and the long walk to church. She had been there—just in case.

She told Grandma and me how they went out for coffee after church, to a diner on Central Avenue. The air was gray and hazy with cigarette smoke, but the coffee steamed up in their nostrils like deep-throated nectar. Gunder, who spoke more eloquently to his tractor than to people, suddenly told Mom of his land and the forecast for rain and the cattle auction next week. My mother, who talked to people all day long, was suddenly shy and listened with wonder at his awkward stories.

She told us how he had dropped her off at the corner near the little alley house. He had looked hesitantly at her and the night, wondering if she'd be safe. But she laughed and said she'd be fine, thanks.

He accidentally touched her hand as they both reached for the door handle, and her hand seemed to tremble, like it was a thing apart from her. She slid out of the car and ran for the alleyway, watching the red taillights of his car disappear down the long street in front of her.

He wrote her a letter that week. It came in the mail, just a plain white envelope with blue ink scrawls tracing her name. My mother snatched it from the windowsill and held it close to her, like it was alive and needed to be protected. She never told us exactly what was inside.

He was coming next week, she announced at the supper table—coming to take her for dinner at the Carolina Pines. She let out a long, shaky sigh.

"Can I go?" I asked.

"No, you can't." Grandma's words darted in, her voice rushed. "You and I'll stay home and fix fried potatoes." That was my favorite.

My mother said nothing, and I wondered why she looked troubled. You should look really excited if you were going to the Carolina Pines. I had heard of it at school since my friend's father worked there. They fixed fried chicken that was so crispy it crackled between your teeth, and the mashed potatoes were so smooth they slid right down your throat. *So why is she sad about that?* I wondered. I noticed that she sat at the table long after supper was over, tapping the plastic table cover with the corner of the white envelope.

I wasn't even home when he came to the little house on the alley. I was roller-skating with Willow, pushing my skates hard up the incline on Fifth Street and sweeping back down like a bird learning to fly on the long narrow sidewalk. By the time I got home, my mother was gone, and true to her word, Grandma had made fried potatoes. Tiny bits of Spam were fried crispy along with them, and I thought it tasted as good as chicken ever could—even at the Carolina Pines.

I was asleep when my mother came home and didn't hear the doorknob twist open, or the quiet whish of my mother's coat as she laid it over the rocking chair—even though I was asleep in the same room. My roll-away bed was in that room, and I slept through everything.

But Grandma's voice came murmuring through my dreams, and then I heard my Mom's voice. "I told him—" I thought I heard her say. There was more murmuring; then she said it again. "I told him about Janie."

I sat straight up in bed. The worst thing I could think

of was maybe I was going to flunk second grade and have to take it over again with that horrid Walter Mason. Why would my mother tell anyone that?

I stared at the yellow and blue flowers on the wallpaper. They swam together, in and out of a thin ribbon of cloud.

"It's okay, Janie." My mother was suddenly there, holding me, laying me back down on the pillow. "Go back to sleep." I felt her body curl next to mine, felt her soft arm across my belly, felt the stifled sob in my mother's chest.

I closed my eyes, but I did not go back to sleep. Not for a long time.

The gray snow of early spring turned to charcoal lace, then melted away to expose infant sprigs of grass and dandelion greens.

"He's probably busy in the fields," Grandma said one morning, seemingly out of the blue. My mother turned to her, the pain clearly in her eyes, and nodded. She dropped her spoon into her half-eaten cereal and left the table. "Well, I wish you'd eat," Grandma said to her, and I slowly finished my own oatmeal.

It was a sadness you could feel, without knowing why—as if the whole world had turned on a strange angle and couldn't right itself. And that had happened, too, in the far-off places where soldiers were dying. We hung a picture of President Roosevelt on the wall, just above the table. We prayed for him every time we said grace. But my mother's mind was clearly elsewhere, roaming around in some other sadness.

It was on a Sunday afternoon when we heard it. A car had pulled up in the little driveway by our alley house. No cars ever came there except Uncle Kenny when he came to visit from North Dakota. We weren't expecting him now. All three of us stumbled to the window to look out.

"Oh." Mom suddenly straightened her yellow Sunday dress, and smoothed down a strand of auburn hair. Then she slipped out the door and down the three steps before Grandma and I could even turn around.

I started for the door, too, but Grandma's strong hand caught hold of my arm. Grandma just shook her head, and I hung back, listening for sounds in the little alleyway.

"It doesn't matter," a man's voice said, and it cracked at the end, like he wanted to say more, but couldn't. "All I could do this whole time was think about you, and I don't care what anybody says about it. It just doesn't matter," he finally said.

"What doesn't matter?" I whispered.

"Hush." Grandma shook her head, and walked out to the little kitchenette. "It isn't right to listen, Janie. Get away from the door."

I stepped back and stared at the door until it became a brown wooden blur. I could hear nothing now, no voices at all. It was as if Grandma and I were the only two people in town, locked in this tiny house by a mysterious silence.

Then the door slowly cracked open, and I saw my mother's shiny face, her nose red like it always got if she had tears in her eyes. Only *these* tears were making her eyes sparkle and dance. He followed behind her, ducking slightly to get through the door.

"Gunder, I would like you to meet Mother," she said, as he stepped forward to shake Grandma's hand. He seemed almost shy, but his smile was warm and engaging.

Grandma laughed her usual little laugh whenever she wanted to be nice, but nothing was actually funny. "Glad to meet you," she said.

"And this is Janie." They were all looking at me now, and suddenly I felt like maybe hiding under the bed. But

I stepped forward and shook his hand, too. It was a big, rough hand, like a tree trunk, but I felt the warm strength of its grasp.

Gunder said he couldn't stay long. He drank a cup of coffee that Grandma had quickly brewed, and gulped down the last piece of rhubarb pie. No one else in the house seemed to matter to him except my mother. "And that's the way it was supposed to be," Grandma told me later. He was making her happy, and she was smiling again, and we needed to be thankful for that.

But the house was lonely after she had left with him. It was quiet and strange, and it stayed that way until she came back later that afternoon, bringing the sunshine swirling in again, with the skirts of her yellow Sunday dress.

CHAPTER THREE

MEETING THE FAMILY

I WAS BUSY AT SCHOOL, learning about the Panama Canal, and I did not see that my mother's heart was not in the Doll House Beauty Salon anymore. I came home from school every day singing, "*Manana, Manana—Manana ees good enough for me...*" I had heard it on the radio, and it made me think of Panama and bananas and a hot, far-away place where everyone danced and sang all day long. I did not notice that my mother wasn't interested in hair shows anymore, or thumbing through hairstyle magazines in the evening.

"Janie," she said dreamily one Friday morning as we walked down the sidewalk on the way to the corner store. She was not working today, as she often did. "Janie—" she suddenly caught my hand. "How would you like to live on a farm?"

I stopped, as if the cement had grabbed my shoes. If there was anything better than a farm, I didn't know of it. A farm, where I could have a cat or dog or maybe even a horse, and a barn, and land where you could see the edge of the sky and run forever on it and never get tired. Or mostly, just have a puppy. I searched my mother's face. *Did she mean it? When could we live there? Now, like tomorrow?* I thought. But she only smiled and tugged me along. "Maybe someday," she promised.

That afternoon, Gunder came by in his western-style pants and shirt with the sky reflected in his eyes. My mother knew he was coming, of course. I should have figured it out, since she spent hours combing her hair and smoothing it with just the right curls swept up from her face and gathered into a bun at the nape of her neck.

The black Plymouth, like an Army tank carrying its commander, rolled to a stop in the little driveway. He stepped out, his eyes smiling and searching for Harriet. And when she saw him, I thought my mother seemed somehow different, like a butterfly just emerged from its cocoon, beautifully perched and ready to flutter away.

"How'd you like to drive into town?" he asked, and I knew that included Grandma and me, though he didn't exactly look at us. He just opened the back door of the

Plymouth and waited for us to climb in. My mother sat in the front, almost like she owned the car, and I fingered the plastic knob that rolled up the back window. I had never been inside a car before, not ever, even though I was already a second-grader, but I mustn't act like it.

We rolled out of the driveway, through the narrow alleyway and onto Seventh Avenue. Gunder drove down Central, and then up a small incline where we stopped for gas. I looked out at the city of Great Falls, seeing it with new and privileged eyes. We drove home again, without stopping anywhere else, but I felt different now, too. I wondered if perhaps Willow had seen me, riding in that car.

Gunder stopped to let Grandma and me get out when we got back home. I stood for a long time at the alleyway, long after the red taillights of the car had blinked up the avenue and turned a corner, taking my mother and Gunder away. They were like the red eyes of some forest cat, blinking, and then they were gone, never to be seen again. I felt my grandmother's presence behind me. "Come on in, Janie," my grandma said. "He's just taking her to the farm to visit his family, and they'll be back tomorrow."

I went to bed that night thinking about Tomorrow. Tomorrow was a Saturday, and if my mother wasn't working, she and I would often go for a walk to the edge of town where you could hear meadowlarks and pick wild flowers. Maybe she would get home in time to do that.

But she didn't. The car pulled into the driveway in the late afternoon, just as Grandma was taking a rhubarb pie out of the oven. "Good timing," Grandma said, and she reached for the coffee pot to get a fresh brew going.

They were smiling as they came into the house. Gunder had his strong arm around my mother's small waist. They both sat down for pie, and Gunder asked Grandma for some Sego milk to pour over his pie. It was as if he had always been there, somehow, eating pie and laughing with Mom and gulping down the last bit of coffee. I hung around the edges, picking up the dishes when they finished eating, and carrying them to Grandma in the tiny kitchen.

Gunder didn't stay long again. He had to get more work done that day, he said. The next day was Sunday, the Lord's day, and he never worked then. He shoved his chair back, gave my mother's hand a quick squeeze, and was gone out the door.

She sat still for a long time after he was gone, not saying a word. She stared across the room as if she was looking out the window, but she really wasn't. I could tell.

"Well, what's wrong?" Grandma finally asked.

"They don't like me," was all she said.

"Who's *they?*" Grandma was not to be dismissed.

"His brothers. And his two sisters visiting from California. With maybe the exception of Ray, the youngest, because I was willing to cut his hair."

"Of course they like you, Mommy, everybody likes you." I couldn't keep out of it. My mother was talking crazy. Who wouldn't like her?

"They don't." She stood up from her chair. "They made it quite plain. They hardly talked to me the whole time, except for Gunder. And Ray, when I cut his hair. The rest just glided in and out of the house like cold fish swimming in a bowl, barely saying a word to me."

I started to imagine fish with hair, staring at my mother and not talking. "And then what?" I asked. I could never wait long in listening to a story.

"Well, you see they have two farms, a few miles from each other. When it came time to go to bed, the women slept in one farmhouse, and the men in the other. They call the sisters from California 'the girls,' and I tried to talk to those 'girls' and get to know them, but it was no use. And it wasn't like they didn't talk to each other."

"Don't sound right," said Grandma.

"It wasn't," my mother said. "I came *this close...*" She held up her thumb and forefinger pinched almost together... "*this close*...to asking Gunder to take me home immediately, and I wasn't coming back." There was a long, stiff silence. "Then I thought..." and her voice grew softer. "I thought they might grow to like me sometime, and anyway, Gunder is the important one. If he likes me, it doesn't really matter what the others think." She said it limply, like maybe she didn't mean it, like maybe it mattered a lot, but the words covered it over like thin ice on a deep, dark pond.

CHAPTER FOUR

GONE

GUNDER CAME TO VISIT AGAIN, not even waiting for the weekend this time. There were special meetings going on at the church and he came down for the Wednesday night service. Grandma let me stay up and wait for Gunder and my mother to come home. She even made another pie to lure them in, but it didn't work. "Well, they got things to talk about," Grandma said at last. "Things to decide on. So you get ready for bed now, and you can listen to the radio."

Grandma and I listened to *The Mayor of the Town,* a weekly show about a gentle mayor who always figured everything out and made it work. *Baby Snooks* came next—that was my favorite—but my eyes were heavy, and I couldn't stay awake to see if my Mom and Gunder had decided anything.

They needed the Mayor of the Town to help them. And then I fell asleep while the radio began to play, "Heavenly Sunshine," and a man's voice boomed: "This is Doctor Fuller, coming to you from..."

I didn't hear another word.

When I opened my eyes, the sun was shining in through the lacy curtains by my bed, and I looked out at a fiercely blue autumn sky. My mother had already left for work, like always, and Grandma was fixing breakfast. No oatmeal today. I could smell bacon and coffee and a hint of fresh orange juice.

Last night seemed like a dream, and maybe it was. But Grandma plunked down my breakfast plate in front of me and said, "Well, they decided something." She grabbed a comb and began to braid my hair. "We have to hurry. You're behind time and this is a school day."

"What did they decide?" I asked, between bites of scrambled eggs. "*Ow.*" I twisted my head, but Grandma continued to French-braid, furiously.

"They're gonna get married this fall, after harvest," she said. "Sometime in October."

"At Halloween?" I asked. That would be a good time to get married, just after I got back from trick or treating.

"No, I don't think so," Grandma said, as she finished my braids, and tied pink ribbons at the ends of them. "I doubt it will be at Halloween."

But, in fact, it was. The day right before Halloween was a sunny day with only a few ashen clouds amid a playful breeze to stir the yellow leaves on the sidewalk by the white church. My mother wore a fitted aqua suit, with a large creamy gardenia corsage. It was the only thing even vaguely white.

I thought she would look lovely in a long white wedding gown, her auburn hair framed by a filmy veil. I had seen other weddings like that. I had even been in one, as a flower girl. But when I asked my grandma as my mother walked down the aisle, "Why didn't Mommy wear a pretty white wedding dress?" Grandma shook her head, and her dark eyes said to never ask that again.

But she was beautiful anyway, and Gunder looked handsome and shy, standing in front of the preacher. Everyone was happy, some wiped tears, and Grandma firmly held onto me and didn't let me run around after it was over. I had to stand quietly behind Grandma in her new navy-blue dress.

We walked over to the parsonage afterwards to have cake and punch and coffee. There were presents, too, for the bride and groom to open. Everyone talked at once, all of them crowded together in the small house, drinking coffee and laughing.

There were also strangers there, strangers who looked like Gunder, tall and sun-burned with eyes as cold-blue as the arctic ice. "They are Gunder's three sisters and five brothers," Grandma whispered. "I met them. Go say hello to them."

But I didn't. I didn't, because they were staring at me. Not in a bad way, though, but like you'd stare at a cat with only three legs and wonder what happened. I twisted uncomfortably by Grandma's side, then slid away to play with two little boys who had wandered by.

But I glanced back at one of the strangers again since his eyes were not blue like the others, but hazel-green. He winked at me. He was young, much younger than Gunder. "I'm Ray," he said to me as I scrambled past. "Gunder's youngest brother."

I stopped then, and stared at him, just like the strangers had stared at me. "I'm Janie," I said slowly, then stopped, because there seemed nothing more to say. The two little boys wanted to play tag now, and I was It.

"What grade are you in?" Ray asked.

"Just started third," I said.

"Me, too," he said, "Just started third."

I wrinkled my nose. "Huh-*uh*—"

"Yep," he said. "Third year of high school. And that over there—" He pointed to another young man who had shocking blond hair. "That's my brother Gordy, but we call him Ole. You'll see a lot of us when you come to the farm because we work there." Then he laughed and went back to his coffee, and I seemed to be dismissed.

The two little boys still wanted to play, but Grandma stopped the game. There was to be no more of this running around. My mother and Gunder were getting ready to open gifts, and Grandma wanted to see. I was to stand still beside her, and be quiet.

But there was nothing interesting in the presents. Only dishes and towels and forks and knives. Grandma said, "Oh that's lovely, that's nice," whenever they peeled back a wrapping to reveal a new tablecloth or lumpy green vase. I kept hoping for some sign of promise in the deceptively wrapped gifts, but they were boring—every one of them.

It was dark when Grandma and I walked home. I had skipped up these familiar blocks until I could see them with my eyes closed, but tonight they were long, and the breeze had turned from playful to mean.

The house was dark, like a small deserted castle, and Grandma fumbled with the key. We walked inside. Grandma switched on a lamp. The foreboding little castle turned into a small, warm house again. Grandma sat down on the bed. "Well," she sighed. "They're gone."

I stared at her. "Gone?"

"Yes, to Seattle. They're going there right away, to Bible school. Gonna study there all winter. Won't be back until seeding time."

Seattle might not have been so far away, but Grandma's worried eyes said that it was. Her eyes said that seeding time was far away, too. I sat down next to her.

"You remember at the reception, her saying good-bye to you?"

I nodded, remembering the too-tight clawing hug, the pin from her corsage sticking into my shoulder. I remembered a warm tear dripping on my neck. "You be good and mind Grandma," she had whispered. "We'll be back as soon as possible." But I had strained to get away, anxious to play again with those same two little boys who were hanging around me.

"She said they'd be back as soon as possible," I said.

Grandma laughed, though she didn't smile. "Soon as

possible's next spring," she said. "When the dandelions come out again."

I slowly undressed for bed, trying too hard to get the buttons on my pajamas straight. I crawled under the covers. The sheets felt like frozen tin. I laid there in the darkness. Grandma was right. They were gone. As far gone as I could ever see.

CHAPTER FIVE

SURPRISES

I WROTE LETTERS. I wrote them in pencil with smudge marks and words spelled funny. I always signed them: "I love you, Mommy. I love you, Daddy." It seemed strange to write "Daddy." I kept waiting for it to feel cozy and right. It would, next time, I was sure. I wrote on little stationery with ducks and kittens on it, the stationery that my mother had bought for me and left with Grandma. Sometimes tears fell on the little page, and I would try to erase them, making an awful wound on the paper, sometimes even a ragged hole, like a bullet had shot through it.

I always received a letter from her, too—every week. It was enclosed in a bigger letter, to Grandma. She told of Seattle, the big, gray city in the fog and the rain, where you could hear seagulls on Puget Sound, and go for a ferry ride. Not at all like Montana. *Not at all.* She and Gunder loved their Bible classes. They were fine. She would write again soon.

It seemed like whenever a letter from my mother came, I would curl up at night with a bad stomachache. If Grandma knew it, she would give me mineral oil, a clear thick oil that coated my throat way down to my stomach and then to my toes. I had seen a neighbor pour oil just like it, only black, down a pipe in his car. So I tried to keep my stomachaches to myself, even if a letter arrived more than once a week, which sometimes happened.

Grandma kept busy with her job at Doctor Layne's house, which was easy since it was only four blocks from our little alleyway house, and she walked there. She cooked and cleaned and took care of their four little boys, all the time I was at school. I would lay beside her at night, and she would tell me about the laundry. "Ten sheets," she would say, her voice tired and soft. "I washed ten sheets today." I'd murmur my astonishment at the number, then fall asleep as she talked about how many little socks she had hung on the line.

As for me, I kept busy with school, and ice skating. I often skated on the pond at Gibson Park, the ice frozen thick and deep blue, with a crunchy layer of frost on top. My skates were like my Bible. You couldn't live without those kinds of things.

And whenever I skated, I told my mother about it in my next letter. She had said there was no snow in Seattle—only rain—and you couldn't skate on rain.

At Christmastime, Grandma and I rode on a train to North Dakota to visit relatives. It was always fun to visit Uncle Kenny, but I wondered out loud to Grandma why we couldn't ride on a train to Seattle. Grandma said it was because there was no room for us to stay there. "Harriet and Gunder have only a small place—smaller than ours—with just one bed." So I slept in my cousin's bed for a whole week and admired their Christmas tree, always feeling like it wasn't ours, even though Grandma said to pretend it was ours, just for that one Christmas.

But winter was good in Montana that year, just the way I liked it. Big wind-carved drifts of snow lay high on either side of the sidewalk. I could run and slide on the leathery soles of my shoes on my way to school.

There was a rule at Whittier School. No snowballs. Anyone seen throwing a snowball would be sent straight to the principal's office, a jail-like room with crinkled glass in the door that you couldn't see through. I heard there were hoses inside that the principal could spank you with. I had tried to imagine somebody getting hit with a garden hose, and it didn't sound possible. But that was what they said. Huge piles of hoses all wound up and waiting to encircle your legs like an angry snake.

I stayed away from the principal's office, tip-toeing silently past it when there was no other way to go. And I never threw a snowball, or made one, even when the snow tried to entice me by forming a sweet wet ball in my mittens.

That was what was happening when Ginger, the Popular Girl, walked by and saw me. "You better not be making a snowball," she warned.

I stood up quickly. "I'm not," I said.

Marilyn, my friend, agreed. "We don't make snowballs," she told Ginger.

"Well, Harold does," Ginger said, waving her hand in the direction of a sturdy boy with curly hair. He was considered the Tough and Naughty Boy. If anyone would throw a snowball, it would certainly be Harold. "I saw him throwing snowballs and he even threw one at *me*," Ginger concluded.

"No,"Marilyn gasped in alarm.

"Yes," Ginger assured us, her chin tilted higher, her eyes narrowed. "Somebody needs to tell the principal."

"Well, *we* will," Marilyn volunteered, grabbing my hand. "Won't we, Janie?" Ginger's approval just hung there, a silent pressure that stifled the air around us. I nodded, pulled my hand away, and crept after Marilyn toward the Execution Chamber.

I didn't go inside, though. I just waited by the door, peeking around the corner to see where the hoses were. They must have been hidden in the closet.

Marilyn walked out a moment later, bravery surrounding her like an aura, a delicious smile on her face. Ginger, a shadowy figure in the hallway, was waiting, too. Together they skipped, danced away, and I followed, my footsteps soft and slow on the polished wooden floors.

When the afternoon classes began, I sat at my desk, puzzling over my arithmetic page. Mrs. Larson cleared her throat. "We have a problem today," she began, from her place by the blackboard. "It has been reported that Harold was throwing snowballs. Would the girls who reported this, or whoever saw him, raise your hands?"

I shot my hand into the air, then looked around. No one else had a hand raised. Not Marilyn. Not even Ginger. Only me. My hand floated down like a deflated balloon. And it was shaking.

"Harold, you need to go see the principal," Mrs. Larson said. Harold scooted back in his chair and plodded toward the door, the condemned prisoner about to face the hoses. And it was my fault. He would get me for this; he would throw a thousand snowballs, all at me—I knew it. I would have to run home from school really fast today.

But Harold was nowhere in sight as I ran the four blocks home to my little house on the alley, my breath coming hard and choking in my throat. Grandma was at the door to meet me. "Why were you running so fast?" she asked, as she pulled me inside. "You might fall down."

I dropped into a chair and kept breathing hard.

"Well, I have an errand for you," Grandma said. "The little corner store is out of milk and we need some for supper. I want you to go to the other store up Fourth Avenue and get some. You know which one I mean. It's not much farther."

I nodded. I'd been there plenty of times before, with Grandma. But what about Harold? I didn't even know where he lived.

"Here." Grandma laid a coin in my hand. "A quart of milk and if there's change, you can get some bubble gum."

The quarter was as cold as ice between my fingers. But bubble gum was magic. It was calling my name: all the way from the store I could hear it, could smell its pink minty sweetness, could feel it large and juicy in my mouth. I had to go.

I even managed to sing as I skipped up Fourth Avenue. "Zippety-doo- dah, zippety-aye. My, oh my, what a wonderful day—" The store man seemed glad to see me and gave me an extra piece of bubble gum as he put the glass quart bottle of milk inside a brown paper sack with handles for me to carry.

I began walking carefully down the street, the sack heavy in my hand. One block. One and one-half. Then I saw him step out from a fenced yard ahead. Big he was—ten feet tall—and staring straight at me. I couldn't get away, not carrying this sack with milk in it.

I stopped still. Harold strode up to me and stood in my path. "How come you said you saw me throwing snowballs?" he asked. "Because you didn't."

I gulped and the bubble gum suddenly seemed huge in my mouth. "Ginger said you were." I was sputtering, the bubble gum in the way. "She said you threw one at her. Marilyn is the one who told the principal, not me." I needed to blame it on somebody, anybody. Maybe I could still escape with my life.

"Yeah, but you raised your hand. You said you saw me."

"I *didn't* say that." I was desperate now, and clunked the paper sack on the sidewalk for emphasis. CRACK! The sound of glass breaking seemed to echo from the nearby hills, from the city, from the sky above. Milk was trickling from the corner of the sack, making a small white pool on the sidewalk.

"You broke your milk," Harold said, his voice softer now.

"I don't care." I swung the sack beside me, the glass tinkling, the milk trailing out in a small bubbly stream. I walked faster, my words echoing behind me, surrounding the startled Harold who was standing still, watching me go.

"I don't care," I said again, over my shoulder as I continued walking. But, of course, I did care. And the closer I came to the alleyway house, the worse it all seemed. What would Grandma say? How on earth could I even tell her? Twenty-one cents gone, just like that—and no milk, either. I took the gum from my mouth and wadded it in its small paper wrapper. Even spilling a glass of milk was a bad thing and Grandma scolded for the waste. What would be the sentence for breaking a whole bottle? I couldn't go home. I would stay outside forever.

I sat down on the steps leading up to the neighbor's house and let the tears fall down my face and onto my hands and onto the wet paper sack with the broken glass inside. I was crying loudly now but I couldn't help it. I couldn't stop.

I felt a hand on my shoulder and looked up into the worried eyes of the neighbor. "What in the world is wrong, honey?" the woman said. But I kept sobbing and choking on my tears. "Here, let me take you to your grandma."

"*No-o-o-o.*" My cries grew louder. The neighbor stepped back and was gone, vanishing like a white rabbit in a blizzard. I wiped my eyes and nose on my coat sleeve, and slunk there, alone.

The neighbor appeared again, Grandma beside her. I felt myself being lifted up by Grandma's strong arms.

"I broke the milk bottle." My tears were coming again, my voice a strangled wail. "It was Harold's fault. He made me do it!"

"Harold who?" Grandma led me inside and closed the door. "Don't worry about the milk. Harold who?"

"Harold in my class." My voice sounded miserable, even to me.

"Well, you tell your teacher." Grandma's brown eyes were serious. "She won't let him be mean to you. And maybe we can even get that milk money back."

I stared straight at the wall. No, we couldn't. And I didn't want to tell the teacher. Grandma didn't understand.

"Do you hear me?" Grandma asked, and I nodded. But I didn't want to.

The next day, I stood at the teacher's desk, one foot on top of the other, staring at the floor.

"Yes?" Mrs. Larson's wide blue eyes were kind, questioning. She waited a moment. Then two.

I coughed and looked away. "Harold made me break my bottle of milk." I said it fast and low, then hurried to my desk and slid in. Mrs. Larson was staring at me, I could feel it.

I looked up at my teacher, who glanced briefly at Harold, then back at me, and started to talk about arithmetic. Suddenly I loved arithmetic more than anything, and I opened my book to the right page. Maybe, by some Irish luck, Mrs. Larson hadn't heard me at all. Maybe.

"I have a little game for you," Mrs. Larson was saying now. "We're all going to make a guess of how many valentines are in this box, and whoever comes closest will get *this*." She held up a large red candy lollipop shaped like a heart, and everyone wanted it.

We had been putting valentines in the lacy box for days

now. I had made my own, a Brownie project that Grandma liked. "Good idea. Saves some money for us," she had said as I colored and glued and made smeary marks on red hearts. Mine wouldn't be as good as some, not ever so good as Ginger's, but there was one for everyone in my class, even a small one for Harold.

"We'll find out tomorrow," Mrs. Larson said, her voice a happy smile. "On Valentine's Day!" It was almost good enough to make me forget about snowballs and bottles of milk. But not quite. I still worried that Harold might be called to the principal's office any minute now, and there would be no redemption this time.

But Mrs. Larson seemed to be unaware of it all. The Valentine's Day party was all that mattered to her—that and taking guesses for the number of cards in the box.

The next day we found heart-shaped cookies and chocolate cupcakes on each desk, and Mrs. Larson served red punch in little paper cups with hearts along the edges. She had thought of everything.

Ginger got to hand out the valentines, and I counted mine. There were thirty-three. One was larger than the rest and had my name printed boldly on the front. I decided to open that one first; no one else had a larger one like that.

A frilly card fell from the envelope into my hand. It had pictures of roses and lace and two puppies in a basket. I opened it and read the verse. It wished me a happy Valentine's Day. A very, very happy Valentine's Day. There were red hearts on the page, flitting in and out of the paper lace. It was signed, "Harold."

I slowly looked over my shoulder to see Harold watching me from his desk, a tiny, shy smile on his face. I felt a burning heat start at my neck and spread upward, and I quickly looked away. But not before I noticed that a stray curl had fallen nicely on Harold's forehead.

The Valentine's Day party was in full swing now, and Marilyn had won the red heart lollipop. But I had a card that I had tucked safely inside my arithmetic book, a card I would keep for a long, long time—maybe forever. And I would show it to Grandma someday, when all this trouble was forgotten.

And then, though it had been long enough that the pain of missing my mother had eased, the snow began to melt in the warming sunshine. It left large puddles under the eaves that the icicles dripped into with a plopping sound. I watched for the first dandelion, pulling apart sprigs of grass in the new patches of snow-drenched soil.

The first one appeared just days before my mother and Gunder drove up in the black Plymouth. I saw the car on my way home from school, when I was half a block away. My legs had never run so fast, exploding beneath me like they weren't even mine. I skidded into the house, and Mom hugged me tight. Everyone was happy and smiling, but something was clearly wrong with my mother. Her stomach was all out of proportion. She was not looking right at all.

I followed her into the bathroom and shut the door behind us. Someone must tell her. "You're gettin' kinda fat, aren't you?" I asked, trying to sound light. I stared at my mother's usual flat stomach, now so round and protruding that she could easily have had a basketball hidden beneath her dress.

She smiled and twisted her head to one side as she looked at me. "Didn't Grandma tell you?" she asked. Then she laughed out loud. "I'm going to have a baby. You'll have a new brother or sister!"

My mouth dropped open and I couldn't speak. No, Grandma hadn't told me. And it *must* be a boy—It just had to be. And I wanted him to be blond and blue-eyed like all the popular kids at school were. And I would hold him and take care of him forever. "When is he going to be born?" I asked.

"In July, about when they're irrigating. And don't get your hopes up about it being a boy, because it might be a girl."

But I said "No, I'm going to start praying right away that it will be a boy." As if that settled things once and for all.

My mother looked at me for a silent moment, as if she were trying to think of something wise and spiritual to say. I think she wanted to cushion my faith, if, in fact, this baby was a girl. But after a while she seemed to give up and decided there was nothing more to say.

That Sunday we all went to church together: me, Grandma, Gunder, and my mother with her large, protruding stomach. The little white church seemed crowded, as if there were a thousand people instead of the 138 the Sunday School register announced from its stand beside the piano. Sunday School attendance: 138. Bibles: 75. Average attendance: 130.

My mother and Gunder seemed almost like returned heroes from a far-off country, like Panama. People stumbled across the aisle to shake their hands, some even ventured a hug. There were delighted laughs and well-wishes for the baby. Grandma smiled proudly, sitting on the end of the pew beside Mom, Gunder next to her, then me beside him.

I looked down the rows of people, past the ladies' black, pin-cushioned hats and the men's round heads, some bald with only a ring of fuzz around the edges. Past them all sat the Newman family—Mom, Dad, and Baby Priscilla, fancy as always in a lacy pink dress and ribbons in her wispy curls. I loved babies and Baby Priscilla was a dream.

It had been only three weeks ago that I had said to Grandma, "Can I go sit beside the Newman's and see their baby?"

"Well, I guess so." Grandma had said.

And I had skipped down the church aisle, astonished that Grandma had said "Yes," hardly believing that I could sit beside Dianne Newman and smile into her baby's wide eyes and touch her chubby hands. I slipped into the space beside Dianne, glanced up at her, then turned my attention to beautiful Baby Priscilla, who grinned a slobbery toothless grin and reached for my face.

Then a coldness descended, like a sour breath that you could feel all over your body. Dianne's face twisted, her lips pulled downward. She jerked the baby around, so all I could see was her soft curls, and she could not see me at all. Dianne reached into her purse and pulled out a rattle for Baby Priscilla. Then she looked back to her hymnal. The music had begun. *"Sing them over again to me, Wonderful words of life..."*

I sat there a moment, my face burning. It wasn't because I looked dirty or ugly—I knew that. I wasn't exactly beautiful, but Grandma always saw that I looked good. I'd noticed my reflection in the mirror that very morning, and my hair was braided neatly, my dress clean, the freckles across my nose not hardly noticeable, and the dimple in my chin looked like a shadow in the morning sun. Why didn't Dianne want me to see the baby? Maybe it was that dimple, or maybe my brown eyes. Most likely it was something like that.

I crept back up the aisle to Grandma, snuggling in beside her, feeling the familiar scratch of her blue polka-dotted dress. I leaned against her shoulder, felt her hand over mine, heard her off-key voice blend in with the rest, *"Offer pardon and peace to all, Wonderful words of life..."*

But that was three weeks ago. It was all different now. I could see Baby Priscilla down there, but who cared? I would have a baby of my own soon—a baby boy, of course—just as cute as Baby Priscilla, and I could play with him all day and no one would think I wasn't good enough for it, even with a dimple in my chin.

And I had a daddy. A *daddy.* Who would have dreamed it? My daddy sat looking straight ahead, listening to the preacher—like I was supposed to, but wasn't. After the singing, everything always got boring. So I kissed his suit coat sleeve, felt his muscular arm beneath the rough tweed. I kissed it again and again. It was like a statue arm, never moving, hardly alive. But it was my daddy's arm. Even if it never moved to touch me. Sometime, it might. Sometime, when everything was all stitched together tight, like Grandma's rag throws and rugs, sewn up and laid straight on the floor. Sometime.

It was a clear, cool night, the stars above set deep and twinkling in the velvet sky. My mother pounded on the door of the little house and woke Grandma and me up. She and Gunder had driven all the way from Conrad, and now they were on their way to the hospital, irrigation work forgotten. Grandma threw on a house-dress, then got me dressed, so we could go along. I crowded into the backseat with Grandma and tried not to hear my mother's soft groans and cries of "Hurry!"

It was much too scary. Something big and terrible was happening. I just wanted to be back in my bed, thinking of school and the Panama Canal. We sat in the quiet hospital lounge, and I clung sleepily to Grandma, who wiped sweat from her forehead, even though it wasn't hot. Gunder sat nervously across from us, staring at the ceiling, then down at his dusty brown shoes.

And then the doctor poked his bald head in the door and said softly, as though someone was asleep, "It's a boy—seven pounds, two ounces. Everybody's fine."

"Oh, thank the Lord," Grandma said, and her hand clasped tight around mine. But Gunder had already disappeared, leaping toward the elevators. "I'll see the baby tomorrow," Grandma said. "And you'll have to wait until she comes out of the hospital, because they don't let kids up there."

"I knew it would be a boy," I whispered. "And he'll be blond with blue eyes. I prayed that, too."

Grandma shook her head. She didn't go much for praying about those kinds of things. "Your mother has brown eyes and red hair," she said, her voice sounding very practical. "So this baby might not be blond at all."

I looked up at my Grandma's dark hair—almost black—and her dark eyes, just the same color as mine. "He'll be blond," I said. "With blue eyes."

And as though some eternal, pre-destined program had

been switched on, the baby had soft blond wisps of hair, and eyes as blue as the Montana sky—as blue as Gunder's. His face was a miniature Gunder, though they had named him John Steven. And I got to hold him the first day home from the hospital.

CHAPTER SIX

CHICKENS, EGGS, AND BABIES

GRANDMA AND I RODE THE GREYHOUND bus every weekend to the farm, to visit. The farmhouse had four rooms, and an outhouse in back. It was lit by kerosene lamps at night, and the water was in a pail by the back door, pumped fresh and cool from the cistern. The house had become Gunder and Harriet's, while the bachelor brothers moved to their farmhouse two miles east. One of the sisters had married three months ago, and the two others were back at their jobs in California. So I didn't have any trouble at all thinking it was my house, too.

There was a school house across the road, white and glistening in the sun, with an American flag whipping in the wind. The teacher's small house sat next to it, two outhouses in back, and a swing with long ropes and a wooden seat. It didn't look anything like my school in Great Falls.

Chickens ran everywhere on the farm, and I tried to make pets of them, until I came across a lame, white rooster that chased me, flying at me in a feathery rage. He became my nemesis, like Captain Ahab's Moby Dick, finding me if I should wander to the edges of the farm buildings, and chasing me back to the house. I saw him come at Gunder once, too, but he just kicked the rooster out of the way, and didn't pay any more attention to it. I knew I could never do that, so the rooster remained a white Evil, lurking around the corners of the granaries or the barn.

He found me once, though, when I was exploring down by the red granary, and I hadn't noticed him scratching there. He began his flapping run at me, but I dove for the rickety stairs along the building's edge. One of the steps was broken and I had to scramble over it to climb higher, scraping my ankle on a large nail.

Moby Dick watched me from a few feet below, while I caught my breath and waited for him to leave. I leaned against the red building, its cracked walls swollen with golden wheat, and smelling hot and earthy in the summer sun. I waited. The rooster glared up at me with one yellow eye, and pranced around, his wings dragging the ground, prepared for take-off if I should step down.

I climbed up the stairway until I reached the top platform. Maybe he would forget about me if I was higher like this. I peeked over the edge at him and he was still there, still cocking his head up at me, that yellow eye keeping watch.

I sighed. If I didn't come to the house by suppertime, they would look for me, surely they would. And by nighttime, he would go to roost and I could come down. But maybe he would stay there for days, eating bugs while I had nothing, and who would ever know? They would search for me along the roads and ditches, the sheriff would come, and I would be too weak to call out, to scream HELP, Moby Dick won't let me go.

I sat up straight and stared back down at the rooster. I was *not* going to starve to death up here on this platform. I started down, one broken step at a time. There was a stick at the bottom, by a clump of weeds, not a big one, but it might do. It was me or Moby Dick. I took a quick leap and grabbed for the stick.

The rooster was there, right in my face, but I flailed the stick at him, screaming "Go '*way!*" and stamped my foot. He came at me from the side, and I swung the stick again, missing him wildly, but he instantly dropped back, like he did when Gunder kicked him out of the way. Just like that.

I was breathing hard and I gripped the stick tighter and glared at the rooster. He suddenly seemed to be looking at an interesting rock on the ground. I turned and walked back toward the house, the stick at my side. Once I thought I heard him coming behind me, the scratching wings on the dirt, the rapid click of chicken feet. But I didn't turn around, didn't even run. And I knew I wouldn't run from him again.

Every day I brought back eggs from the hen-house, and set them in a bowl on the kitchen counter. "How many eggs does a chicken lay every day?" I asked my mother one morning. "A dozen?"

"Oh no," she answered, laying baby Johnny in his tiny bassinet. "I don't think more than three or four."

Gunder was there, smiling in the kitchen, and then he poked the man standing next to him, a neighbor who was drinking coffee and talking about the weather. They both stopped and looked at her for an amused moment. Then they walked outside, and I could hear them laughing.

Grandma turned from the sink where she had been doing dishes. "A hen only lays one egg a day," she pronounced, looking straight at her daughter. "I thought you knew that."

"How was I supposed to know?" she said.

"Well, you'd better learn these things." Grandma wiped the soapy bubbles from her hands on a dry dish towel. "If you're gonna live on a farm, you have to know something."

"We had thought that we might *not* live on the farm," my mother said, her voice suddenly serious, and as heavy as cement.

There was a silence in the kitchen and it brought a chill, like the winter wind. Not live on the farm? How could she say that?

"That's why we went to Bible School all that time I left you and Janie. Gunder wanted to see if he should be in the ministry. It wasn't so far-fetched. His father had been a Lutheran minister. And we both felt that the Lord had a special calling for us, beyond the farm, perhaps." She suddenly whirled around and grabbed a cloth to wipe up a coffee spill on the counter. Her eyes were bright and the chill was gone. "But Gunder doesn't feel he is quite up to it. And his brothers expect him to keep farming. So—how many eggs does a chicken lay, now?"

Grandma laughed then, and I relaxed. My life on the farm was no longer in jeopardy, though I had never known that it had been. And my mother had wanted it to be, clearly she had. I could see it in her eyes, a wistful look that begged for something to be different.

"It's just that I don't fit in here," my mother said.

"Yes, you do," Grandma said quickly. "Or you will, soon."

"I don't think so." She leaned back against the cupboard. "They act like I'm from Mars, instead of Great Falls, for Pete's sake."

"You have to give it time, Harriet." Grandma was wise and always right, and she knew it. "These things take *time.*"

"Just because I don't say *ain't.*" My mother wasn't listening. "You have to say *ain't* around here."

"I say *ain't,*" I said suddenly. "I started saying it soon as we came here."

"Well, you can stop," she said. "I don't want to hear you say it again. It isn't proper English."

"Nuthin' wrong with a good word like ain't," Grandma grumbled as she walked away. Grandma said "ain't," but she didn't try to be proper like Mom did. She didn't spend a lot of time reading books, or even trying to write poetry. So "ain't" was okay for her. It wasn't okay for me, my mother said. Wasn't okay for her, either. The two of us would not say "ain't."

But I said it whenever she wasn't around, so I could sound like I really belonged on this farm. "There ain't no more eggs in the chicken coop," I yelled to Gunder one day, as he was clumping toward the hen-house in his big irrigation boots. "I got 'em already." And he nodded and turned back toward the barn, like he understood me just fine.

❧

THE GIRLS ARE COMING. My mother said it softly, but her voice had shivery echoes. I remembered from school that "the British are coming" was a scary thing to the colonists. Well, it was that way now, just about. The "girls" from California were coming. They came once a year, only during summer. But Harriet was in a panic, snatching up every stray toy and swooping down upon the kitchen floor with her mop. I kept Johnny outside under the trees, while her cleaning frenzy rolled through the house. And when the girls finally got there, I spoke politely to them, and held Johnny close to them so they could admire his wispy hair and sky blue eyes. Then the visit was over, and Mom sat in a chair and fanned herself. I stood nearby and wondered how my mother could become so unraveled over it.

After all, she had told me the tragic story of the Pearsons. How, in North Dakota, their minister father had died suddenly of a ruptured appendix, leaving his wife and five children, another on the way. How she had remarried, had three more children, then lost that husband. Not long after, she had died, too, and nine children were left to care for themselves, and they did. The oldest raising the younger ones until all were grown, undaunted and bravely loyal to one another, but not knowing the comfort of a mother's arms about them, nor the sweetness of laughter. Just survival, desperately scraping for it in the Depression.

Hard work drove them, hard work and no time for play, nor letting someone else in to ease the pain. That was the reason for their aloofness, Mom said. That was why. Besides that, they were Scandinavian, not known for warmth. But still, the frosty mist that seemed to follow them settled on my mother, dampening the fire of her spirit, making her into some shaken woman that I didn't know.

Maybe it was good that they lived in California, I thought. My mother did perfectly fine with the ones who lived nearby. She especially liked Gunder's sister who farmed with her husband a few miles south. They all farmed, in fact, minding their own business, mostly, only occasionally clomping through the kitchen for coffee. Two of the brothers had farms of their own, and Gunder farmed in partnership with the oldest Pearson brother, Bernhard.

My mother knew, and I sensed it, too, that Bernhard was the top man on the Pearson totem pole, no matter what. His word was final on any subject around the farm. To me, he was a large man, looming mysteriously around the fringes of the place, stepping into the kitchen for a silent cup of coffee, then plodding back to his truck to zoom back to some important task. He lived in another farmhouse two miles east, with Ole and Ray, and Ray's dog, Cubby.

Up until now, I hadn't seen that much of Ray on the farm. Maybe it was because he and Ole were busy in the fields with the other men when I was there. But now, every weekend when Grandma and I rode to Conrad from Great Falls, Ray was there to meet us in his jeep at the Conrad Hotel, which was also the bus depot.

He would swing our suitcase up and over the side of the jeep, then climb in the driver's seat. Grandma would sit in the front, and I would sit in the back where there was no roof. I loved it. The wind blew my hair straight up and then to the side, whipping it sharply against my face.

"Ray drives a jeep," Harriet explained, "because he wanted

a jeep, and after all, he's the baby of the family. So he finds every excuse he can to drive that jeep to town." And I was glad, because I liked nothing more than riding in that jeep. I got to ride in it home from the bus depot every Friday, and back again on Sunday afternoon.

And Ray was fun. He and Ole weren't like the older Pearson brothers. They liked to tease me and say funny things. Once Ray hoisted me on his shoulders and ran around the outside of the house, all around in a circle, trying to keep away from Cubby.

Cubby was a black Lab mix, friendly, and completely devoted to Ray. He was nice to me, too, wagging his tail against my legs, but always on the alert for Ray's voice—for his command to "siccum" or to fetch a stick. "Never say 'siccum' to Cubby if there's a chicken around," Ray said. "He ain't supposed to chase them, but sometimes he forgets, especially if you say 'siccum' and he don't see anything else to chase."

But I did say "siccum" one day to Cubby when Ray wasn't around, and Moby Dick was. Cubby tore after the rooster so fast that I felt sorry for it and screamed for Cubby to come back to the porch. He did, dropping and panting beside me, and looking around guiltily to see if Ray was near. Ray came outside then, and nobody said a word. And

I decided right then and there that someday I would have a dog like Cubby, all my own. A dog that really belonged to me.

Johnny was growing, walking now, though he was not quite a year old. His blond hair hung fine and straight across his forehead, but when they went to town, Mom would form it into a long curl across the top of his head. His blue eyes would crinkle when he saw Grandma and me get off the bus. "Hello, Angel," I would say, every time, and Johnny would laugh when I picked him up.

My mother was sick again, vomiting whenever she smelled food. Grandma complained about it to me, when Mom couldn't hear. "As if she don't have enough to do," she said in a worried whisper.

"She can't help it if she's got the flu," I said.

"It ain't the flu," Grandma said, and that was all she was going to say. It wouldn't do to ask her more.

But I soon figured it out. My mother's stomach started to grow fat again, while the rest of her kept as slim as ever. "Another baby," I said deliciously to myself. "And it will be a girl."

It seemed to take longer, this time. The summer dragged by, Grandma and I coming up every week-end on the bus, with Ray to meet us, and Johnny to hug when we got to the farm. And Harriet's stomach kept getting bigger and bigger.

"It will be a girl, you know," I said one day to Mom and Grandma. It seemed they looked at me with more respect, and didn't try to tell me different. "And she'll be blond with blue eyes. I prayed it." They looked at each other, and not at me.

"Go outside and play, Janie," my mother finally said. "Maybe Gunder will let you help him milk the cow."

But I didn't ask him that, because he wouldn't. I'd already asked once before, but Mom didn't know it. "Naw," he'd said, and didn't give a reason. But Ray let me help, whenever he milked the cow. I'd walk out with him to the far pasture where the milk cow would hear us coming, and then we would start back. The cows would plod along behind me and Ray would answer all my questions about cows and chickens and dogs. He even added other explanations. "Bernhard and Gunder don't think women and girls should do chores like driving a tractor or milking the cow, especially if they don't know how."

"But I want to," I said. "It's not fair."

"I know," Ray said, "but you should be glad. Don't want too much."

We walked along silently for a moment, until Cubby barked at the cow that seemed to be veering off the worn path.

"The only thing I really want," I said, "is a dog like Cubby."

"Well, there ain't no dog like Cubby," Ray said. "You gotta train 'em, work with 'em, gotta keep at it. They ain't just born like Cubby."

I was quiet, and stared down at my feet, avoiding the fresh cow pies. I had already asked my mother if I could please have a puppy, asked her a long time ago, when we first came here. Ray didn't know that, of course, but I was certain that I would have a dog someday. And I would make him like Cubby. I would.

CHAPTER SEVEN

BOOTSIE

HE WAS A SCROUNGY PUP, white, with brown spots on his legs. "You can call him Bootsie," my mother suggested brightly, watching me jump up and down. "I *told* you we had a surprise for you when you got off the bus!"

My mother said 'we,' but I knew right off that Gunder had nothing to do with it. He ignored the pup like he wasn't there. And Grandma plain didn't like him. Mom's eyes sparkled, and she let baby Johnny touch the puppy's soft ear.

"I gotta train him," I said. "Gonna make him just like Cubby."

"Don't know what you got a dog for," Grandma mumbled. "You got enough work, with Johnny and a new baby coming."

"Oh, we just picked him up at the pound there in Shelby," Mom said, as if Grandma had asked where they got him. "He'll be a nice puppy for Janie."

"She's never here, except on weekends, and you gotta take care of him in the meantime."

My mother pressed her lips together and turned away. So Grandma stood up, reached for a broom, and started sweeping the floor, like she always did when she was upset.

I carried the pup out the door and set him in the grassy weeds just outside the front porch. "You're my dog," I whispered in the pup's ear, while he lapped at my face. "Just don't get too excited and jump up on Johnny and knock him over. I wouldn't like that. You gotta get trained."

But Bootsie *was* excited, and he growled and tugged on my sweater and ran around in circles. "*Stay,*" I commanded, and Bootsie ran faster, until he stumbled on his own puppy feet.

It seemed like I was the only one who liked Bootsie. Well, my mother did, sort of, but she was much too busy with Johnny and the housework to do more than scrape some leftovers into a dish outside and hope that Bootsie got it before the chickens, cats or even skunks discovered it.

When I came up to the farm on weekends, I noticed that Bootsie was quickly getting bigger, now too large to carry around, and he still wasn't "trained." I tried again. And again. Bootsie couldn't learn much, I decided. But I loved him, anyway. I drew a heart in red chalk on his patch of white fur.

That was so I would recognize him in Heaven. There must be a lot of dogs looking like Bootsie up there.

Ray asked me once what that red mark was on the mutt, but I didn't tell him. He didn't like Bootsie, either, mostly because Bootsie would bedevil Cubby, trying to hang on his fur and growl and play, like Cubby was his mother. Ray didn't like that much, and kept kicking Bootsie off Cubby whenever he was around. Bootsie would yelp and run to me, and I consoled him in my arms while he licked my face.

But I could only be there part of the time. I didn't know what was happening while I was in Great Falls. I did tell my friends that I had a dog on the farm, and his name was Bootsie. All my friends admired me for it.

One day Grandma said she couldn't go to the farm that weekend. Doctor Layne was out of town and Mrs. Layne needed her to take care of the boys. I felt my heart turn over, and unwanted tears spring to my eyes. I blinked them furiously away. "But your mother said you can come by yourself," Grandma said. "I can put you on the bus here tomorrow and they'll get you there. I don't like it one bit, but that's what they said."

I whirled around the tiny kitchen. "*When?*"

"Friday," Grandma said, her voice suddenly sounding tired. "And that's tomorrow, so we'd better get you ready."

The next morning, Grandma and I rode the city bus to the Greyhound bus station, like always. The bus was idling there, its engine like a purring cat. I climbed on board, only pausing to give Grandma a quick kiss on the cheek.

I looked around to see if anyone was there whom I might possibly know. There wasn't. Only rows of people who were reading, some were smoking, some were talking and no one was looking at me. The front seat was empty, so I slipped into it. I was quite alone now, and did not feel grown up at all like I'd expected. I looked out the window at Grandma, who was waving good-bye, a white hanky laced in her fingertips. I might not do this again. But the farm was waiting. I had to get there.

I waved back desperately at Grandma's worried face until the bus backed out of the alleyway that was the Station, and pulled out onto its usual route. I knew it by now, knew which street the driver would stop at and look both ways before easing onto Central Avenue. Then past the Civic Center and Gibson Park. Under the viaduct and out past Black Eagle. On the way to Conrad.

But I was so very alone, and no one to talk with. No one at all. Maybe I could talk to God, I thought. I looked out the window at the twisted rows of strip farming that carved into the gently rolling hills. "Hi God," I said. "I'm kind of lonesome."

It was all I said. A Presence hovered around me, as suddenly as a flash of angels' wings. God was here. He had somehow got on the bus and had sat down beside me—a little girl, whom some people didn't even want to sit beside in church. I couldn't see Him, but His glory was all around me. Even the blue-green seats, so scratchy and pungent with tobacco smoke, seemed sacred now, and what could I do about it? I dropped to my knees. It was a bus rolling down the road, and no one must see me, but I was small and who would notice? My tears dropped on the seat, and I didn't even know why I was crying. Finally I sat back up and looked out the window at all the wonders that this Presence sitting beside me had made—the sky, a soft evening lavender with streaks of gold and orange, and the wheat fields running away to the edge of the green velvet hills. I sat quietly, not wanting to disturb anything. It must never leave me, this feeling of the Divine presence beside me, so close, in fact, that it seemed a very part of me.

And now, Conrad beamed its twinkly eyes at me as the bus drove over a small rise, and the twilight sky was almost purple. This time it wasn't Ray who met me, but my mother and Gunder and little Johnny.

I climbed down the steps of the bus, ran to them with wild hugs, then turned all my attention to Johnny, grabbing him up and kissing his round cheeks. My fingers sifted through his blond silky hair. "Hello, Angel," I said, and squeezed him again.

My mother laughed. "We ask Johnny—what will Janie say when she gets off the bus? And he says, 'Ho' Ango'."

We all laughed then, and I marveled to myself how smart he was, and how he could talk and remember that I called him "Angel."

But then the laughter stopped, too soon, and Mom's face became sober. "Janie, I have to tell you," she said, "and I don't like to—but Bootsie isn't here anymore. Bernhard had to shoot him."

"*What?*" I leaned against the shiny black metal of the car, feeling its cold seep into me. *"Why? Why?"*

My mother reached into her pocket for a tissue and handed it to me. "We were in town yesterday, Gunder and I and Johnny, and when we got back, Bernhard said he had to shoot the dog. Said he was chasing after a chicken and killed it."

My sobs became louder, and my mother said, "Sh-h-h-h, now, Janie. They say if a dog ever kills a chicken, he just won't stop. They have to shoot them."

"I could've stopped him," I wailed. "I could've!"

But we were in the car now, and it didn't seem right to cry out loud anymore. I leaned my head against the window and felt Johnny's small soft hand on my shoulder. My sobs grew further apart in the stillness of the car. And that feeling I had on the bus that God was with me? It hadn't gone away. It was still there, even now, like warm honey pouring over me, touching the sad place, making me stronger.

I was glad now that I had put that red chalk mark on Bootsie's leg. Someday I'd see him again Up There, and he'd run to meet me and lick my face, just like before.

CHAPTER EIGHT

THE BIRTHDAY CLUB

IT SEEMED LIKE EVERYBODY KNEW about Bootsie. Ray came over with Cubby for a while, and they were quiet, and didn't want to play. I stayed outside most of the morning, poking around in the grove of trees next to the house, imagining Bootsie was with me.

Mrs. Moore, from the next farm to the south, brought over a plate of anise cookies, tiny and rich and speckled with seeds. She handed them to my mother, with a sad, sideways smile at me. "Next time our cat, Sweetheart, has kittens," she said, "I'll just save you one, Janie. In fact, you can pick out whichever one you want."

And then the day seemed to start over, the sun sweeping out from behind a cloud, and skipping on the leaves of the trees. I could think of nothing better than a kitten, and I wished it was born today, this very minute.

"Thanks for the cookies," Mom said, placing them on the small kitchen table. "These are really good. I want the recipe."

"Well, I made these for Birthday Club," Mrs. Moore said, her voice bright. She knew they were good, no doubt about it. "I had so many left over."

"What's Birthday Club?" my mother asked.

"It's just a get-together once a month for the farm wives. We celebrate whoever's birthday is that month."

"That sounds fun," Mom said. "I'd like to do that."

"Well—" Mrs. Moore paused, and I wondered why. She should say, of course you can, Harriet, of course you can. But she said, "You know, it isn't up to me, wish it was. But I'm going to ask, and I'll let you know. I'll let you know real soon. I'm sure it will be fine."

My mother went humming around the house after Mrs. Moore left, happy as if she'd been invited to Willow Burg's birthday party. I followed around after her, carrying Johnny, and then sat down with him in the living room's overstuffed chair that smelled of tractor oil and hired men, and read to him, "The Three Bears." It was Johnny's favorite. Mom cleaned the floor around us, still humming, until the faded linoleum seemed to come to life again, its yellow and gray rectangle shapes dancing beneath her scrub rag.

"Janie, it's a good thing the bus doesn't leave until 6:00," she said, her humming suddenly over. "You can go to the Sunday School picnic with us tomorrow."

"Where's it at?"

"At the old Armstrong place, they said. They have a lot of trees out there. I'm bringing chicken and a potato salad."

And then, as though the Birthday Club was already forgotten, my mother's next job was to start on the potato salad. I got to take Johnny with me and go out to search for eggs. "We need about six to ten," Mom had said, and I was sure I could find that many. The chicken coop first, then the stray nest over in the machine shed.

When I came back with the eggs, Johnny was holding a brown one in his warm little hand, and Mom was ready to put them in a pot with boiling water. The potatoes were peeled and cooked next. I hung around the fringes of the kitchen, finding entertainment for Johnny with a spatula and a pot lid.

A faint knock quivered at the kitchen door. Johnny heard it first, then I followed him, just as Mrs. Moore poked her head around the screen door. "Oh good, you're home," she said, but her face didn't say it. She leaned against the wall for a moment, staring down at my mother's freshly mopped floors. "Harriet, I'm awful sorry I have to tell you this, but I ran into Mrs. Scott in Ledger a little while ago. Told her about you wanting to join Birthday Club?" She hesitated. "And she said she thought they had enough members already now, what with me joining last and all. But I told her you would have made a good member. I told her that."

My mother didn't say anything, not for what seemed to me, 'way too long a time. "Oh, it's okay," she finally spoke, looking up from her pot of potatoes. She even smiled. "I don't need to belong."

Mrs. Moore's face relaxed into a smile then, too, and with a promise of more anise cookies to come, she was quickly out the door, and gone.

And then my mother dropped the bowl of unfinished potato salad down on the counter and it slid away from her fingers. She leaned over it for a moment as though trying to pull her life back into place. And when she turned around, I saw the tears, though she was wiping them away with the palms of her hands.

"I'm gonna tell Grandma," I said.

"No, you're not going to tell Grandma." Her voice was even, now, the horrid moment past.

"But you wanted to belong to their stupid Birthday Club, and they should let you. They should! Why don't they?"

My mother breathed in a long sigh and began stirring the potato salad. "It's hard to say, Janie," she finally spoke. "But I don't really want to belong to their Birthday Club. Not anymore."

Yes, you do, I thought. But I didn't say it.

ꕥ

I had my little suitcase packed, my clothes rumpled and smelling of barn, and a small box of anise cookies for Grandma tucked inside. Gunder put the suitcase in the trunk of the car, so that after church and the Sunday School picnic, we could go straight to the bus depot.

I sat next to my mother and Gunder on the hard wooden pew and listened to the sermon. Sometimes I glanced around the church at the worn, earnest faces, the dust of the farms still clinging to their clothes. It was like opening a picture book and looking in, wishing to jump inside and be part of the book. But I closed it, keeping my finger in the imaginary page in my mind, and leaned against my mother's slender shoulder. She looked straight ahead and seemed almost—like now—to belong in the book.

We stood in long lines at the gray, wood-planked table under the Armstrong's cottonwood trees, and waited for the last platter of fried chicken to be carried out. Pastor Williscroft had already asked the blessing, a long one, invoking God's blessing on the food and the Armstrong family and the missionaries, all the missionaries. My stomach was growling and I knew I could eat at least half of my mother's potato salad.

But by the time I came to the salads, hers was gone, only a tiny glob of potato left in the bowl. So I took two pieces of fried chicken, far too many baked beans, and a huge chunk of dark chocolate cake before I left the serving table and ran to sit beside my mother and Gunder. Johnny was on his dad's knee, already chewing on a drumstick.

They had announced the games, and some people were lining up for races. Mom handed her plate to Gunder. "That's the ladies' race, I think," she said, peering across the yard. Several women were gathered there, and a teenage girl, too tall for her age, was drawing a line in the dirt.

"You can't run in this, Marvel," someone hollered at the girl. "You'll beat everybody."

"No, this is for married women," Marvel said, with a bright smile, because she was in charge of the games, and she was good at it. "All married ladies," she called out, looking around at no one in particular.

"Well, that's me," my mother said, her voice proud as though she was announcing it to the whole world. She bent down to give Johnny a kiss on the top of his head.

I looked at her, at the growing bulge under her loose-fitting maternity blouse. You can't do this, I thought, and my voice in my head sounded like Grandma. Everybody knew my mother couldn't sprint. Well, Grandma and I knew it. She would dash off in a burst of speed, but she ran funny, kind of pigeon-toed, and not going very fast at all. Uncle Kenny used to tease her about it, and she'd say, "Well, I hate races, but I could probably beat you." And then they'd laugh because they knew she would never run in a race. But now she was walking across the yard, smiling and laughing with these good church people, like she had known them forever and at last belonged somewhere in that picture book.

They lined up, someone hollered "GO," and the women were off, all six of them, like race horses clawing the ground. My mother was the auburn one, the beautiful mare with flying mane. But around the corner, on the rutted race track, she twisted her foot and fell headlong in the dirt. A little cloud of yellow dust surrounded her and when she tried to get up, she cried out.

I could have swallowed my tongue; I felt like I was going to. I stared at my hurt mother, wondering at the feelings inside. "It isn't worth it," a feeling said. "You are better than all of this." But tears froze up my vision and I could barely make out Gunder lifting her from the dirt and carrying her to a chair. I ran over and stood there, hanging onto Johnny, who kept trying to climb onto his mother's lap.

Beulah, who was a nurse, got ice from the ice cream maker and packed it around Mom's foot. Mom was trying to be brave, like it didn't hurt much, but I knew better. Her face was pale and she couldn't wiggle her foot at all. The picnic was over.

I had to get on the bus with the image of my mother's face like an instant snapshot in my brain—her face still tinged in pain, but with a hopeful smile, saying good-bye. The valiant, gentle face. "We'll see a doctor tomorrow," she whispered to me. "Don't worry."

But I worried all the way to Great Falls, where I collapsed in Grandma's arms and told her the whole dreadful story.

Grandma's lips formed a straight line. "We'll go up there next Friday, soon as you're home from school," she said. "I'll see what I can do about it."

CHAPTER NINE

LUTEFISK

IT WAS A TORN LIGAMENT, the doctor said, and my mother either had to stay off it or get crutches. So she got crutches. She was there with Gunder and Johnny to meet Grandma and me when we climbed from the bus, and she looked brave and fresh in a clean maternity blouse, and big crutches under her arms.

"Gunder doesn't go to doctors much," I heard her confide in Grandma. "But this hurt so bad, he took me to town first thing on Monday morning."

"I should hope *so*," Grandma said, with a sideways glance at her son-in-law. "Probably couldn't get your washing done, either."

"Gunder helped me," Mom said. "But there's a lot more to do."

So Grandma turned into the Laundry Management Authority as soon as the car stopped in the gravelly driveway and her suitcases were carried to the bunkhouse. Gunder started the wash machine—a gas-powered metal box that shuddered and clattered like a disabled war plane trying to take off. It spewed evil fumes in the east room of the bunkhouse so that I could scarcely breathe. But still, I wanted to help in this mysterious ritual of clothes washing. It seemed like much more fun than going into the house and sweeping the floor, which is what Grandma told me to do.

"Oh, honey, why don't you just read to Johnny and keep him occupied while I start dinner," my mother said, taking the broom from my hand. She reached for a small worn book from the bottom shelf of the bookcase and handed it to me. It was my book, "A Child's Garden of Verses." She smiled when I recognized it.

"We have to start reading poetry early," she said, "and Johnny's not too young."

I remembered her reading all these poems to me—and more besides. "Can I read him 'The Highway Man?'" I asked, scanning the shelf for the old poem book.

"No, he's too young for that one," Mom said from the

kitchen. "Just read him the others. We have to start with Robert Louis Stevenson."

And Johnny snuggled close beside me, his eyes wide and staring at the page as I read, "*How do you like to go up in a swing?*" I was sure, though, that he could have understood "The Highway Man."

"Well, one good thing," my mother said at the dinner table, as she passed the dish of boiled potatoes to Grandma. "We don't have to fix dinner tomorrow. We're invited over to Munson's after church. For lutefisk."

Grandma almost dropped the dish of potatoes. "Lutefisk?" She asked, as though it were a word one must never say.

My mother laughed right out loud and Gunder grinned. "Yes," Mom said. "Gunder loves it, and I remember eating it as a child at Grandma Olson's in Canada. I think I liked it."

"What is it?" I asked.

"Nuthin' you'd want to eat," Grandma whispered to me, but they all heard it and laughed some more. Grandma was not Scandinavian, and she didn't care.

But I was instantly curious. It seemed as though lutefisk was suddenly a secret code word that could get you on the inside, another notch closer. I could hardly wait to try some. But Grandma sat there, quietly eating her meat and potatoes and saying not another word about lutefisk.

But she did, the next day, right after church. We were all in the black Plymouth on the graveled road that turned off the highway. The Munsons seemed to live a long way from town.

"Gonna try some lutefisk?" Gunder asked Grandma, his eyes teasing.

"Nope," Grandma snapped back. "Wouldn't touch it. Not fit to eat."

"What *is* it?" I asked again. "I want some."

"It's cod fish soaked in lye then boiled 'til it's slimy," Grandma told me. "It tastes terrible. You don't like onions and they're good for you. Why would you eat lutefisk?"

"It's not that bad, Janie," Mom said from the front seat. "You'll see. And, Mother, they'll have potatoes and probably Swedish meatballs, too, so don't worry about it."

"I ain't worryin'," Grandma lied. She always worried, and everybody knew it.

But she needn't have worried about food at the Munson's. The tiny kitchen glowed with the warm smell of home-made rolls and freshly brewed coffee. The table was already set, and food was being carried in. I looked hard for the lutefisk and finally saw what must be it, a platter of unfamiliar-looking glutinous hunks of white fish, steaming and letting off a metal-like smell. A bowl of melted butter was set by it, and I thought *that* looked good.

They all gathered around, and Mr. Munson said grace in Swedish, with Gunder echoing a loud "amen."

I felt as though I was doing something distinctly naughty, taking a good helping of lutefisk. Grandma was glowering at me, and I knew it. Grandma didn't want to be the only one not eating it, but she was.

I poured the hot butter on it, and took a bite. It slid down my throat, wriggly and slippery, like it was alive. I poured more butter on and tried again. This time I could actually taste it. It was better with a big mouthful of potatoes. And somehow I finished every last bite.

"Look at that!" my mother exclaimed. "Janie ate all her lutefisk!"

Suddenly, all eyes were upon me—blue, approving eyes.

"I want some more," I said, reaching for the nearby plate of jiggly fish. I heaped a large slab of the lutefisk onto my plate, poured butter on it, and wondered how I would ever get it down, now that everyone was looking at me. But I took a bite—lutefisk, butter, potatoes, cream gravy—and down it went. By the time I finished my second helping, no one was caring anymore. But a miracle had occurred. I actually liked it. I leaned back in my chair, full, and complete. I had somehow finished a rite of passage, one that Grandma could never imagine.

CHAPTER TEN

THE MOVE

I DIDN'T KNOW WHEN I would ever eat lutefisk again. Certainly Grandma wouldn't fix it. My mother would have to learn. And that might take a while, with everything else she was learning.

It was getting harder for her to lift the laundry now, or even Johnny. Her legs were mottled with varicose veins. "It's all those years in the beauty salon," I heard her say to Grandma. "On my feet, all the time." She wouldn't say it was also because she was pregnant again, and no one else said it, either.

She came to Great Falls to have the baby, in the same hospital where Johnny was born. It was late in the fall, the harvest already safely finished. One morning early, as soon as the first pains came, Gunder carried Johnny to the car, then ran back for my mother and her suitcase. They took Johnny to the little house on the alley, then drove straight to the Deaconess Hospital.

Gunder didn't come back to the house for a long time. I sat in a corner on the floor and read to Johnny. Every few minutes, Grandma strode past and pulled the curtain back to peer out the window. "Don't know why he ain't back yet," she'd say. "It's been forty hours."

"Not forty hours," I corrected, looking up from my book.

"It seems like it," Grandma said, then looked out the window again.

He did finally pull into the little driveway, and step into the house, his eyes red-rimmed from lack of sleep, but his teeth shone white in his tanned smile. "It's a girl," he announced. "Eight pounds. We named her Nancy Marie. And Harriet is fine."

Grandma collapsed into a nearby chair and sighed. I pulled Johnny closer to me. "We have a new baby sister," I whispered in his ear, but he was still too interested in his book and handed it to me to read again.

Gunder didn't stay long, just giving himself enough time for a cup of coffee and three doughnuts that Grandma had bought yesterday at the store. He had to get back to the farm and help Bernhard fix a combine, he said. Johnny would stay the two weeks with Grandma and me, until Mom and the new baby could come home from the hospital.

I could just imagine this new baby. I was so excited I could hardly stand it. Nancy Marie would have lots of blond curls and big blue eyes. Surely she would. Then she would be the most popular girl in her fifth grade class, when she got there, with those blond curls and blue eyes.

One of the best things about having this baby was that Johnny got to stay with us and he was there every day when I got home from school. And one day when I ran up the steps to the little house, Johnny met me at the door. "Bee Bee. Bee Bee," he told me, and led me to the little pink bassinet. He stretched on his tiptoes and pointed at the tiny bundle.

My mother hovered nearby, and pulled the blanket from the tiny face. The baby had full, round cheeks, a small heart-shaped mouth, a round nose that turned up, her eyes tightly closed in sleep. And no hair. The blond curls were simply not there.

"Johnny had quite a lot of hair when he was born," she said, as if reading my mind. "But Nancy's will grow."

I sure hoped so. I ran my hand over the tiny bald head. Nancy was like a real live baby doll. There was fuzz on her head, though, and I looked closely. It was blond fuzz. I smiled to myself, filled with the knowledge that all would be well with this baby. Then I grabbed Johnny's hand and led him outside. We would run to the corner store for a candy bar, to celebrate.

~

That winter was the last I would spend with Grandma, though I didn't know it then. On most week-ends, Grandma and I would board the bus, and begin our two-day sojourn to Conrad.

Two days were enough for Grandma. She would do the laundry every week, basket after basket of sheets, diapers, dresses, coveralls. She hung them on four rows of cold wire line in the back yard. Hours later she would carry them in, stiff as frozen hunks of long white fish. I laughed to see Gunder's long-johns, standing alone like a rigid ghost, and Mom would dance a little jig with them in the kitchen.

I stayed inside, reading to Johnny, holding Nancy, trailing my mother around the kitchen, helping to fix dinner. Two days were never enough for me.

I sensed Grandma's fear, especially at night. Grandma would tuck the covers around my neck, then lie down in the bed we shared. Sometimes I dropped right to sleep, and sometimes I lay staring into the darkness, wondering why Grandma was still awake.

"You don't want to go stay there," Grandma said to me one day, as though we had both been thinking the same thing, but I hadn't been. "They'll make a hayseed out of you."

"What's a hayseed?" I asked. If it had anything to do with the farm, I figured it was good.

"It's somebody with hay growing out their ears, because they don't know anything but living on a farm."

I could see myself, long strips of yellow straw protruding from my ears, and folding back into my braids. "That wouldn't be so bad," I told Grandma, and then laughed as though it were of no consequence at all, when Grandma clearly thought it was.

It was in the early spring when my mother first mentioned it to me. It was a Saturday morning, and Grandma had to stay in Great Falls, so I was there alone. The sun was shining, but the ground was still dry and frozen, with little cracks opening up like thirsty mouths. "Janie," my mother said, "Would you like to go to school there across the road next year?" She nodded toward the one-room school-house across the way.

I had already explored the school, soon after I came. I thought it lucky to have a school, with books that maybe I could borrow, so close by. But it seemed quaint compared to my big brick school in Great Falls. There was only one swing in the yard, and two outdoor toilets, one for girls and one for boys. A tiny house for the teacher sat next to it, with a very nice lady named Miss Walker living inside. She had shown me the inside of the school one Saturday, weeks ago, when I had wandered over there. Even though it was only one room, the paper-pulp smell of books, the dusty chalkboard, and the huge globe on the teacher's desk made me know this *was* a school, for sure, and it might be a good one.

I looked over at my mother and shrugged my shoulders. "Well, you go think about it," she said, "and then you tell me your answer. You can live here on the farm, or you can keep staying with Grandma, whichever you like."

I walked slowly over to the school yard, to the swing, which hung limp and worn and inviting. I draped myself across it, belly first, and watched the brown dirt and dry yellow weeds move back and forth before my eyes. How could I even answer my mother? What about Grandma? This was too hard.

I whirled the swing around and around until it was tightly twisted. Then I let go and spun. The school-house, the farm, the earth and sky, all blurred into one and became the very breath in my mouth. Great Falls seemed far away right now. How could I not choose the Farm? But the thought dragged a pain through me, gray and heavy as a rusting hulk, and I knew I'd have to carry it for a long time.

My mother smiled when I told her I chose the farm, and hugged me close. "I knew you would," she said, "but I wanted the choice to be yours." I couldn't explain about the iron weight inside me, so I didn't say anything.

"As soon as school's out, we'll move you up here," she said. "And Grandma, too. She can live in Conrad. There are a lot of little apartments around town." That was the only thing that could nudge the iron weight, and it did, just a little.

But Grandma didn't want to hear about moving to Conrad. "I can't move there," she said. "I got my job, working for the doctor."

"Oh Mom—" Harriet tried to argue. "They can get someone else to take care of those boys and help in the house."

"They pay me good," Grandma said. And that was the end of it. Grandma didn't like change. She never liked to move, and the thought of leaving the little white house on the alley was just too much.

I tried to talk to her about it every day, but she had closed herself up inside somewhere, so that when I looked into her eyes there was a wall behind them that shut me out. And that's when the iron weight lodged itself deeper in my belly, so deep I felt it could never move.

School was over on a Friday afternoon, a day that had breath like a thousand wild flowers. Grandma had quietly packed my clothes in a suitcase, and my books and toys in a large box which she bound with white cord. I watched her silently. She didn't even jump up and run to the window when the gravelly roar of a truck engine rolled up beside the house.

"They're here," Grandma said, and we both waited for the door to open and my mother and Gunder to step inside. Mom was bright and smiling, and helped to carry things to the truck, lugging them over the side like a practiced stevedore.

The piano was the hardest. "You could leave that," Grandma said to no one but the moon. The piano was my mother's, her most prized possession. She had bought it to replace the xylophone we'd had in our other little apartment in Great Falls. One had to have music. I would take lessons one day, my mother had promised. But for now, the piano was moving to the farm. Just like I was.

A couple of neighbors from across the alleyway strolled over to help move the piano. And while the adults struggled with the instrument, clinking and twanging its reluctance, I ran over to the corner of the tiny yard and leaned against the fence. That iron weight was making my stomach hurt, really bad. I vomited into the grass, then kicked dirt over the spot. No one had noticed. I wiped my mouth and walked slowly back toward the truck.

Grandma wiped tears with a large white hanky when the piano was finally in the truck, bound down and covered with a dusty gray burlap tarp. The piano had been the final bastion in a battle she had clearly lost. The piano would not be back. And neither would I.

The long drive to the farm, which had been so much fun on the bus, now seemed long and jolting, with suffocating dust flying in the open window. I had to throw up three more times, with Gunder skidding to the side of the highway, and I tumbled out, spraying the weeds and black asphalt with my yellow strangling vomit. Once I got it in the truck, and Mom couldn't clean it up because it made her gag, too. So Gunder had to do it. I would have been embarrassed, but I was too sick to care.

And when I finally got to bed that night, on the pulled-out purple sofa, the covers tight up to my ears, I dreamed I was back in the little house on the alley. Grandma was there, telling me I had become a hayseed and was giving me some mineral oil to make it better.

CHAPTER ELEVEN

EARL'S BULL

MARGARET WAS MRS. MOORE'S DAUGHTER; two years younger than I was, but almost as tall. I liked her instantly because we had one great thing in common: We both loved cats. "Sweetheart had kittens, you know," Margaret told me, "and we were going to give you one, remember, but the tomcat got 'em and killed 'em all."

I shook my head in horror. Maybe it was some other animal, like a coyote. But no, Margaret insisted, it was the tomcat, because they do that sometimes. But Sweetheart was pregnant again. So I could still have a kitten, as soon as they were old enough to give away.

Margaret told me of dangers I hadn't thought of, not in Great Falls. The farm was supposed to be where the earth awoke each morning, ready to burst into life, and the breezes rustled the leaves of the trees.

There shouldn't be any dangerous shadows here. But there was, Margaret said.

There were rattlesnakes. You should never just walk along, like you were on a sidewalk in town. No. You had to look down and walk, down at your feet. You never looked around, only down. And you listened. If you heard a whirring sound, you knew you were in trouble, and you'd better run. I ran from many whirring grasshoppers until Margaret told me that rattlesnakes sounded *something* like that, only different.

And there was Earl's bull. Earl Sprague, the neighbor, had a bull which by all accounts was the most fierce, savage creature ever seen. And he sometimes got out of his pasture and roamed around, looking for children to kill. When Margaret came to play, and we were catching frogs in the pond or pretending to have a circus, Margaret would hear a snuffling, or a pawing, or a snorting, and suddenly whisper, "Earl's Bull!" And I would scramble after her, up to the hay loft, or to the house, barely escaping in time. Only I never saw the bull.

I began to wonder if there really was such an animal or if he was as big and mean as Margaret said. I never said that to my new friend. I just thought it. And then one day when Margaret was visiting, we wandered down past the barn to a nearby machine shed. I'd been there lots of times. An old brown hen laid brown eggs there instead of the hen house, and I would run there to check on eggs. This day we were simply wandering, dreaming up a new circus act that we could do. We rounded the corner of the machine shed, and there, as if poured with molten iron and planted directly in our path, was the towering black hulk of a bull. His rump was toward us, but he slowly turned his massive head and looked at us with red eyes, red like the fires of hell.

My heart pounded, I could hear it, and my mouth was dry. "Margaret," I whispered, and reached for her. But she was gone, and I hadn't heard the slightest footstep. I couldn't move for a moment, but kept staring at those red eyes, until finally I could turn and run, my hair flying straight behind me. I stumbled into the house and slammed the door behind me. My breath was like the pounding in my chest, hard and heavy.

Margaret was there, trembling in the corner of the room. Mom looked at me, her brown eyes questioning, though I knew Margaret must have already told her. "Earl's bull!" was all I could say, and pointed in the direction of the barn and machine shed. Then I leaned harder against the door.

My mother didn't seem quite as afraid as I had thought she would be. "Well, he won't come in the house," she said, and pulled me away from the door. "Leave the door open, honey, it's hot in here. We'll just use the screen door."

I looked at the regular door, then at the screen. It was bulging in places. Earl's bull could poke his horns right through that.

"We'll tell Gunder when he gets home for lunch, and he'll take care of it."

But Earl's bull was gone by then, disappearing into the shimmering summer afternoon, as though he had only been a mirage. Margaret and I didn't see where he'd gone, and we'd watched, too, from different windows in the house. And I wondered if my mother believed there'd been such a bull, the way she told Gunder about it. Margaret had already gone home by then and couldn't confirm my story.

But now I knew that I must practice being like an Indian, and I did, until I could feel it deep down. I watched, with darting black eyes for bulls, and listened for rattlesnakes, with my ears that could hear a strange rustle from the grasses in the next village.

❧

The day the kitten came was one of those mornings when I thought I'd heard a rattlesnake down by the barn, and was up at the house now, playing Ring around the Rosie with Johnny and Nancy. Mrs. Moore and Margaret pulled into the graveled driveway, and Margaret jumped out, holding a small black kitten with a white nose, mewing and clinging to Margaret with tiny outstretched claws.

"It was the only one we could catch," she said. "There are five others, one all white, but we couldn't get them."

"This one is beautiful," my mother said, as she pried the squalling baby from Margaret's dress. "Look at the little white nose."

"It's like a white star," I said, as I touched the kitten's nose.

"Yes," Mom said, then placed the kitten in my hands. "You could name her Twinkle." My mother always liked to give names.

"Yeah," I said. The kitten was quiet now, in my arms, and I patted the soft black fur. "Twinkle."

The name having been bestowed, the kitten settled in my lap. Mrs. Moore and Margaret quietly left, with Margaret promising to come back in the afternoon. I played with the kitten for a long time, letting her crawl across the room, tentatively exploring every corner. She lapped some milk I had set down, then sneezed and looked up at me with milk droplets trembling on her whiskers.

"I *love* her," I said.

My mother nodded. "She *is* adorable," she said. "But you know, Gunder doesn't like animals in the house, only when it's storming or really, really cold outside, like in a blizzard."

"He'll never see her inside," I said, and I knew it was true. When Gunder came in from the fields, Twinkle would go outside.

"People here think cats are only for catching mice in the barn," Mom said. "They don't keep them in their houses, like people in Great Falls do. You have to understand that. This is your pet, but she's a farm cat. Anyway, she'll love to be outside—kind of like you."

I looked up at my mother and shrugged. It didn't matter much where Twinkle lived. I would be close by.

Fortunately, Twinkle made herself at home in the patch of sunflowers that grew right near the back door. I could always find her there, stretched out in a little sunny spot. Her food dishes were nearby, but Twinkle had another diet: grasshoppers.

She would leap into the air after them, causing the sunflowers to sway and bend. For every time she missed, she caught one. Then she would crunch it down, and mew at me as if to say: "Get me another one." I could have, but I didn't. It was too much fun watching Twinkle get her own.

I did sneak her into the house sometimes, but the kitten was growing now and getting more difficult to hide. And Johnny and Nancy loved her too much. Johnny would carefully stroke her fur, but Nancy would grab the cat by the neck with both hands and toddle around with her in a strangle-hold.

"*No-o-o,*" I screamed one day and rushed to the rescue. Harriet only smiled as I dropped Twinkle outside into her sunflower patch.

"Man, that was a close one," I whispered to Twinkle, who shook herself and ran off lopsided into the sunflowers.

~

Ray was there the morning It happened, a morning so clear and full of promise, the air a breath of fresh sweet alfalfa. He had stopped in for a cup of coffee and some elusive part for a tractor. "Wanna see my kitten?" I asked, and he said, "Soon as I finish my coffee." He didn't seem that interested in kittens, but he and Mom followed me outside, Johnny and Nancy toddling behind.

Twinkle was lying on her side in the sunflowers, breathing hard with strangled mews coming from her throat. I reached out to grab her up, my eyes already stinging with tears. "What's *wrong?*"

"Don't touch her, honey," my mother said. "She's very sick."

"Got a poisoned grasshopper, looks like," Ray said. "She's a goner."

"What's a 'poisoned grasshopper'?" I said, my voice too loud. "Somebody help my cat!"

Ray shook his head. "She ain't gonna make it," he said. "You know that red wheat down by the granary that you're not supposed to get into?"

I nodded, not even trying to stop the tears. I knew about that poison wheat. I never went near it. "But cats don't eat wheat," I said.

"Yah, it's supposed to kill mice and rats," he said, "but sometimes grasshoppers get into it and eat it—then that makes *them* poison to cats. We had some cats die from that last year, over at Bernhard's."

It was like he was talking about the weather, when my little cat was suffering, breathing her last. I stood there, unable to move, until the kitten shuddered and lay so still that I knew Ray was right. She was dead. She didn't have a chance.

I turned away and ran behind the bunkhouse, where weeds sheltered a spot near a small irrigation ditch. I could cry loud here and no one would know. I leaned against the bunkhouse, and then slid down its scaly side until I landed in a heap in the weeds.

I was still there, crying as loudly as I could, when I felt a hand on my shoulder. I looked up and saw the Ray the Weather Reporter. He lifted me up and said, "C'mon, we'll bury your cat." He had a shoebox in one hand, a box that had contained a pair of my mother's shoes. I scrambled after him, scratching my legs on the thorny weeds behind the bunkhouse.

He picked up the shovel leaning against the house, like it had always been there, but he must have had to find it somewhere. "Get some sunflowers," he said, and I dutifully picked the biggest and brightest I could see—a whole bouquet of them, sticky and odorous in my hands.

Then I trudged after him along the cow path behind the barn. Ray was talking. "We can have a funeral," he said. "Ever been to a funeral?"

I shook my head.

"Well, they sometimes sing. Wanna sing?"

I shook my head again. "No."

"Thcy preach. Wanna preach?"

"No."

"Just bury the cat?"

"Yes," I said, fresh tears springing.

"Life is like that," Ray said, suddenly sounding like a preacher, himself. "Things die. All living things." We had come to a sweet green field of new mown alfalfa, and climbed to the top of a little rise. Ray began digging a hole in the earth, just big enough for the shoe-box coffin. "But life goes on," Ray said. "The sun comes up. Another day. Another chance to love another cat. It just goes on, Janie."

I nodded, and stuck the bouquet of sunflowers, wilted now, on the top of the little grave. I was still crying inside, deep sobs heaving like an underground earthquake, but I dried my face with the palms of my hands, and turned to leave the little grave, with one last look. Twinkle would have loved the sunflowers there. It was right.

CHAPTER TWELVE

THE HAIL STORM

GRANDMA AT LAST DECIDED TO MOVE to Conrad. There had been much urging going on, I knew. Grandma had moved into the doctor's home, occupying the room in the basement that had been Grandpa Layne's. She worked hard, cleaning, cooking, and taking care of the Layne boys. But everything was different now—strangely different.

Whenever I visited her, I realized that Grandma's room was only hers now, not mine, too, as it had always been before. It was an odd feeling of separation. I wondered if it was because I had been adopted now. It had happened so suddenly. One afternoon, we had all gone to town and stood in front of a judge at the courthouse. Gunder had repeated some words after the judge, and the man even asked me some questions about how I would like being a Pearson instead of an Olson. Oh, it was fine with me, just fine, I had said, and everyone smiled. And like that, my name was changed and it was no longer the same as Grandma's. "She will always be your Grandma Olson," Mom had said to me. "Always. Nothing has changed." But it seemed like it had, like I was wandering in a far-away field, not an Olson anymore, but not quite a Pearson, either. Just wandering around in that far-off field.

But now my mother had found a small apartment in Conrad for Grandma on the second floor of an apartment building, where other older people lived. The side window looked onto an alley and the north window looked over the scraggly yards of some farm businesses—as well as the church where we went every Sunday.

Grandma's apartment had only one room—a place for the bed, a dresser, her rocking chair and sewing box. In the opposite corner of the room was a small table and two chairs, a sink, a small gas stove and a little refrigerator. Next to that was a closet. There was a bathroom down the hall.

And Grandma was truly happy, at last. She felt safe, even though her knee hurt her when she climbed the stairs. She was content, as though she had finally found the place that was right for her, the little spot to call Home. I could visit her often, and Grandma could come to the farm, too, every Monday to wash clothes.

It was on a Monday like this when the Storm came. The day had begun like a beautiful hot summer day should—the birds twittering their concert in the trees, the clanking of heavy machinery from some far corner of the farm. Harvest hadn't quite begun, but the anticipation ran high.

The wheat was thick and tall. Only just yesterday, on the way home from church, Gunder had driven around from field to field to look at the wheat. At one point, he stopped the car, and everyone tumbled out—Gunder, Mom, me, Johnny, Nancy and Grandma.

We stepped out into the field (not too far—rattlesnakes, Grandma had reminded us). And I could hear them, too, whirring all around me, getting ready to strike. But they soon turned into grasshoppers.

The wheat rustled and whispered in the hot afternoon breeze. We had stood there, the wheat up to Gunder's waist and to my armpits, and my mother took a picture with the new camera. "It's a bumper crop," she had said, and Gunder nodded. Not many crops like this were seen in Montana. And Mom didn't have to say more. A bumper crop meant a new car, a new tractor, and a new washing machine.

But this was Monday now, and Grandma was in the bunk house, wrestling with the *old* washing machine. Gunder had to start it because no one else could. And when it started, it sputtered and roared like always. The whole bunk house vibrated and filled with fumes. At noon, I had to yell at Grandma and tell her it was time to eat.

"Just go ahead," Grandma yelled back, over the top of the wringer. "This is my last load, and then I'll quit." The rest of the wash hung brightly on the lines outside, the warm breeze flapping up the sheets, and making the diapers wave like hundreds of little white flags.

"Okay," I said, and walked toward the house, Johnny hanging onto my hand. I did notice some clouds in the hot summer sky, over there by the mountains. But they were a long way off, and the wash would be dry long before they could ever move overhead.

But as the afternoon sun crawled slowly toward the mountains to the west, the clouds began to swirl closer, and the breeze turned cold. Grandma and my Mom ran for the wash outside, bringing in armloads of fresh smelling clothes, dumping them on the bed and racing outside for more.

I kept Johnny and Nancy inside, by the corner in the kitchen, where there was a yellow rocking chair. I sat there with Johnny on one side, and Nancy on my lap, and read "A Child's Garden of Verses." It was as though no women were sprinting past, calling and shrieking and trailing wash cloths and small socks behind them as they ran for another armload, racing the clouds and the big drops of rain which were surely coming. I would have joined the race, but "keep the babies out of the way" were my orders, and I was following them, secretly glad that I didn't have to get wet.

The clothes were piled high on the bed now, the overalls on top, because they were the last to be washed and weren't quite dry yet. But the laundry was the last thing on anyone's mind.

They all stood on the front porch, looking up. I looked up, too, and saw the dark, rolling clouds, wickedly purple and tingeing out to green at the edges. But the biggest cloud was frosty white and luminous, standing out in stark contrast. That was the one we were staring at. Staring at in fear and disbelief.

Grandma headed everyone inside, just as the first pings bounced on the roof. Even Cubby came inside, nervous at this unexpected privilege. The pings soon became a roar, like a trillion hammers pounding the house to the ground. And then the front room window crashed in. Shards of glass and ice skidded across the floor.

"Quick," Grandma shouted, "Everybody hold a pillow to a window!" Grandma hated storms more than anything, I knew, but she was an expert. She'd grown up in Minnesota and had a storm cellar there for really scary storms. Now I wished I had one, too. A place to run for safety.

Instead, I jerked a pillow from my bed and held it tight against the bedroom window. The pounding continued, and I could feel the force of the hailstones against the glass, against my pillow. But I couldn't reach the pane above my head, and I felt the crack as the glass exploded around me, the hail free now to fly inside, hitting the dresser, and bouncing on the linoleum.

"Get away from the window, Janie." Grandma was there, hollering above the roar. "It's okay. Just let it go."

I hugged the pillow to my chest and ran into the kitchen. My mother and Gunder were there, standing quietly in the middle of the room, Mom holding Nancy, and Johnny clinging to Gunder's leg. I raced around them, and dropped to my knees beside the yellow rocking chair. "Oh God, save us, save us," I prayed as loud as I could above the clattering on the roof. Cubby crept up beside me, whining in his throat, and pushed his black head under my arm.

I could hear the pounding grow fainter, ever so slightly. Then, as I was still on my knees, it began to subside, like some monster lady at a dance, picking up her clattering skirts, and tip-toeing away. It was over.

I stood up. A cold breeze hit my face from the broken kitchen window. Glass and hailstones lay shattered together on the floor, the ice beginning to melt in round little pools. Grandma was already sweeping it up, ordering me to take Johnny and Nancy to the front bedroom where there was no glass broken. "Keep them in there," she said, her voice high-pitched and anxious, "'til we get this all swept up." My mother was helping, picking up a large shard between two slender fingers.

Gunder stood there in the front bedroom too for awhile, staring out across the fields. I could see from the window how the golden wheat that had stood so proud and high yesterday was all hunched over and flat, unable to rise again.

We stood there alone, only the two of us in the room now, the voices of Mom and Grandma and the kids floating softly from the living room. The noise of the season's hours; the tractors' roar; the rush to the fields at dawn; the laughter at the table—all melted together and became the sodden, beaten mass before us.

There were really no words to say. I just knew we were mourning the beautiful wheat together—Gunder and I.

Then words did come, though I didn't know how. "I'm sorry—Dad," I said softly, almost choking. "I'm so sorry." He nodded and I saw the sudden tears that welled in his eyes. He sighed then from somewhere deep inside, and stepped out the door to look up at the sky.

A few moments later he was gone in the pick-up, gone somewhere "out east" to see how Bernhard's crops had fared. They were sure to be all right, Mom had said. The storm was here. But he had to find out for himself.

Now they would probably have to borrow from Bernhard to get through another year. I could hear my mother explaining this to Grandma. But give up on the farm? "Oh no", she said. "Gunder would never do that. Never."

And hours later, when he finally came back inside, I knew it was true. There would be another spring, another day to plant, then to harvest. It was all there, settled in his steel blue eyes.

CHAPTER THIRTEEN

THE MYSTERIOUS TABU

I STARTED SIXTH GRADE AT PIONEER SCHOOL that year. The school had a little porch in front, just big enough for stomping off snow from boots. The teacher's desk was in front, a blackboard across the wall behind. A flag hung limply to one side, well away from the furnace. An aging piano was on the left, and a ping-pong table in the back. Rows of books covered the right-hand wall.

I was glad the school was just across the road, because I could run home at noon every day. There was just enough time to eat lunch and read a story to Johnny and Nancy before running back across the road. School had never been better.

When the teacher worked with the first grader, I listened carefully. It would be so much fun to teach someone to read. Margaret, the fourth grader was next, then Sonny

Rogers who was in the fifth. At last I had my turn with the teacher, then Joan Rogers, who was in the eighth grade.

I knew I was still "the girl from Great Falls" though, because they had to show me things, like how to play "anti-i-over" over the school house. I couldn't imagine throwing a ball over the roof of my brick school in Great Falls. I'd be in the principal's office with those hoses if I tried it.

Winter bore down on us, stiff winds from the north with nothing to stop them tearing across the plains, sending drifts of snow across the roads and molding it into glistening white mounds around the edges of the farm.

The schoolhouse was always warm, the furnace giving off throbs of heat from its iron belly. Just after Thanksgiving, wires were strung across the front of the room, with white sheets hanging down. Practice for the Christmas program had begun, taking precedence over all else.

I had sweaty palms and shaky knees the night of the program, because twenty-five people had crowded into the schoolhouse, sitting in the desks and on rows of benches in the back. I was in three short plays and had a monologue. The white sheet curtains were drawn back on their safety-pin runners, a chord from the off-key piano was struck, and Christmas began.

When the program was over, Santa Claus clomped in from the snowy outside, with a loud "Ho Ho Ho" and a white pillowcase full of candy treats slung over his shoulder. "It's my dad," Margaret whispered to me. "He's always Santa Claus, but don't tell, 'cuz nobody's supposed to know." I nodded, seeing George's familiar eyes behind the round glasses. For now, he *was* Santa Claus, and that's all that mattered.

We walked home later that evening, Dad carrying Johnny, and Mom holding Nancy, with Grandma and me between them. "Be careful not to fall," Mom said, and Grandma answered, "I won't," like she never did, but sometimes it happened. I held her hand more tightly. I looked across to the house, to the Christmas tree shimmering in the front room window, the moonlit tinsel sending whispers of silver across the drifted snow.

Winter pounded the northern plains like a wild man with a frosted hammer, wind screaming out of the north, snow scuttling across the roads and fields.

Dad stepped in the back door one raw morning, kicking the snow from his boots. "I been over to Clint's," he said. "They said it's 50 below out. Don't feel like it."

I was just slipping my arms in my coat, ready to head for school. "Run fast, Janie," Mom said, and I did, although I agreed with Dad. The wind had died down, and it didn't feel like 50 below. I took a deep breath and it went clear to my lungs, like an icy stab, pure and clean. The sun was shining, pale and cold in the sky, but making the frost sparkle on the bony tree limbs, like a thousand twinkling diamonds.

I didn't even want to go inside the schoolhouse; I just wanted to stay outside and breathe the air and see the trees in their white dressing gowns against the blue of the sky. When I opened the door of the school, warm air enveloped me, like the arms of a worried mom, hurrying me inside. The furnace was roaring, and classes were about to begin.

During eighth grade History class, Miss Walker remembered that she had left some graded papers on her table in her little house. "Janie, would you please run over and get those?" she asked me, as I studied my sixth grade math. "They're on my dresser."

"Sure," I said, feeling lucky because Sonny Rogers obviously thought *he* should get them. Even a fleeting moment of freedom was not to be taken lightly.

I stepped inside the teacher's house, noting the neatness of the place—a contrast to our house where toys and clutter abounded. Except when Grandma was there. But Miss Walker had nothing to disturb the perfect order of her tiny kitchen, with its table and chairs and small stove.

There were only two rooms. I stepped into the bedroom and immediately saw the papers on the dresser. And then I saw the bottle of Tabu, sitting beside the papers. It was inviting me to try it, to put some on my wrists and behind my ears, like it was meant to be. The smell was strong and spicy, more pungent than I had expected. It filled the air, circled around all the corners of the room and curled up onto the ceiling.

I ran to the kitchen and pumped cold water over my wrists. But that only seemed to make it spread, like some terrible leprosy. Vaguely, the Bible verse, "Be sure your sins will find you out" trailed across my brain. I had learned it in Sunday School at age seven. This was surely what it meant.

I walked back across the crusts of snow as slowly as I could, hoping the cold would somehow freeze off the vapors of Tabu and send them floating to the sky. But when I entered the schoolhouse, I knew that hadn't happened.

I placed the papers on Miss Walker's desk and quickly slid into my seat and grabbed up my arithmetic book. Sonny Rogers twisted his head to look at me and whispered loudly so everybody could hear: "*What's that smell?*"

I felt my face grow hot. I glanced over at Miss Walker who was looking back at me, a tiny smile beginning at the corners of her mouth.

"Janie got into Teacher's perfume," Sonny spoke again, louder this time. He was laughing, too, as if to say, "You should've sent *me*, Teacher. This is what you get."

Winter left slowly, like a reluctant beast forced from its lair by a soft sweet note of spring. The meadowlark sang it first, from a grainy fencepost by the school. Then a few wild flowers appeared, and suddenly the men were in the fields, the winter wheat was green, and Miss Walker left the schoolhouse windows open. The sound of far-away tractors, the earthy smell of tilled soil, and the fragrance of Margaret's bouquet of lilacs on the teacher's desk were too much for me. I gazed out the window and sighed.

Then the last day of school arrived. Miss Walker brightly suggested that we go on a field trip that day, and it could be our choice. She hadn't expected that we would want to catch frogs, of course. But what could be more of a field trip than running across a field to some remote reservoir to catch frogs? Joan Rogers said she would only go along to walk beside Teacher and Punky Reed, the first grader. Sonny, Margaret, and I were off like horses at the starting line. Bernhard's reservoir was hidden in a far-flung field; only cows knew where it was. Cows and me, that is...

The water was warm and brown, and soon we were slopping in the mud and slimy moss, grabbing after each fat frog before it plopped into the water and disappeared into the murky depths of at least two feet. The frogs seemed to always escape, though, even the ones we were able to keep in a bucket for a few minutes.

I was mostly concerned with wearing Sonny Rogers' watch while he caught frogs. It was quite an honor, not to be taken lightly. The heavy thing hung on my wrist and was keeping me from really entering into the frog-catching business. "Don't let it get wet," Sonny had told me as he slipped it onto my wrist. And so I couldn't. And that one frog that Margaret missed? I could have caught it.

But summer was just beginning. There would be more cloudless days like this, the sun hot on my back, more reservoirs to slosh around in, more frogs, and I wouldn't be wearing Sonny Rogers' watch; it would be just me and Margaret and we would build a frog city. It would have canals to swim in and frog grocery stores and dress shops.

"Okay, time to go," Miss Walker said, way too soon, and we traipsed back to the school, always watching the ground for rattlesnakes.

CHAPTER FOURTEEN

SAYING GOOD-BYE

THE DAYS GREW LONGER AND HOTTER, grasshoppers whirred in the fields, and mosquitoes hummed all around and settled like clouds over the farm. It was harvest now, the busiest time of all. Combines roared in the distance and trucks rolled past, heavy with grain, leaving billows of choking dust behind them. Men came in from the fields, faces sweaty and dirt-caked, sloshing their greasy hands in the washbasin and drying them on an already dirt-streaked towel, before sitting down to eat fried steak and boiled potatoes, with side helpings of fresh peas and corn for lunch. My mother did most of the cooking, but Grandma helped, too, whenever she was there.

She came often, because Mom was pregnant again and had varicose veins. We were counting the days until the baby was due, sometime around the end of September. Nancy would be two in November, and Johnny had turned three in July. Grandma shook her head at it all. "I guess some people don't know when to quit," she whispered to me one day. But I just stared at her, not knowing for sure what she meant. I only knew that Grandma was desperately worried about Mom, and the furrows on her forehead seemed to be getting deeper whenever she sighed.

School started again, before harvest was finished and before I was ready. My mother sat on a stool every morning with me on a small chair in front of her while she French-braided my hair. Then I jumped up and ran for the door, because I always waited until the last minute to get to school. "Come straight home," she said before the screen door banged shut. "I need your help with the kids."

I had just got home from school the day It happened. It was a day like all the rest; Mom busy in the kitchen making a spice cake, Nancy tugging on her skirts, and Johnny trying to climb up on the cupboard. I swooped him off in one arm and swung him in a circle. Then I picked up Nancy and kissed her round, sun-chapped cheeks.

We heard it at the same time, the truck roaring into the driveway. My mother instantly dropped her stirring spoon and ran outside. That was not the way Dad drove in.

He rolled in quietly, down by the old garage, so as not to awaken the kids if they were napping.

It was Tony, Dad's younger brother, his face twisted in some kind of pain that I didn't recognize. "Is Gunder around?" he hollered at my mother. She shook her head "No," then Tony slumped against his truck. "There's been an accident out east," he said, "and somebody's been killed. I don't know who." He didn't have to say that it was probably one of the Pearsons. His face told her that. And Dad wasn't "around." He was "out east," helping to get Bernhard's harvesting done. "I'm goin' out there," Tony said, then drove away in a cloud of dust.

My mother stared after him, the spice cake now forgotten. "Out east" meant out east of Conrad, of course, where Bernhard had some good land. It was about fifteen miles away. It might as well have been fifteen thousand. I stood on the porch, feeling like I had turned to stone, my mouth open at the news, and not able to close it.

My mother shooed me back inside. "Just keep the kids entertained," she whispered. "Read to them. Anything." I led Johnny and Nancy to the living room sofa, where books lay ready. Mom finished the spice cake, and its warm aroma filled the kitchen. A good, sweet smell in the house which had suddenly become as eerie as a tomb.

The cake was done, and now my mother began furiously sweeping in every room, whipping the throw rugs outside. Finally she sank into the yellow kitchen chair. The paralyzing thought that her husband might be gone hung in the air, unspoken, but permeating every silent corner.

Even the children were quiet, listening big-eyed to the Three Bears, as if for the first time. Flies bumbled along the windowsills, and usually Mom would have swatted them, every one, but now she sat stiffly in the chair, her round stomach curving against the tent of her maternity blouse. She sat there for hours, it seemed. Hours. While I read on, and Johnny fell asleep against my shoulder.

The sun was dipping closer to the glistening ridge of the Rocky Mountains to the west when a truck rolled into the driveway, and a man climbed out. A man in familiar overalls, with sunburned face and earth-soiled hands. His head was drooped almost to his chest.

My mother flung the door open and ran to him. She clung to him, sinking her face into his shirt, holding him close. I stood in the doorway, Nancy on one hip. "*It was Ray.*" I heard his voice, strangled in his throat. "Driving a load of wheat to town and a guy driving a truck passed another truck when he couldn't see for the dust. Hit Ray head-on, and they say he died instantly. Other guy's not hurt." Then, as if the news was too much for even him to comprehend, he stopped talking, and headed for the house.

I stood out of the way, and leaned against the wall, while Nancy slid out of my arms and ran for Mom. The room was silent, and I stood there, ramrod straight, as if glued to the wall. I had seen Ray just yesterday, his hazel eyes crinkling at the edges when he laughed and teased me and told me that he had only one more year of school left, and I had a hundred and eleven. He showed me how to throw a stick into the trees so Cubby would fetch it and maybe get the wrong stick because there were so many, but he never did. That's how smart Cubby was.

I jerked open the back screen, let it slam behind me, and ran for the bunkhouse. I flung myself across the bed in the room Grandma and I shared whenever Grandma was there. No one was there now.

I waited for the tears to come. The same kind of blood-hot tears that scalded my face when Bootsie got shot and my kitten died. Those kind of tears. But I stared up at the peeling walls with eyes as wide and dry as the cracked ground outside. If I had tears in me, they were stopped up inside somewhere, swelling and creaking, and slamming against my chest.

The funeral was on a hot afternoon, the sky a blue shroud. The men should have been in the fields, finishing up the harvest, driving in the grain, laughing and joking over dinner, drinking gallons of coffee. Instead, they were lined up silently outside the church, waiting their turn to file inside to the front pews reserved for them.

Grandma was caring for Johnny and Nancy in her little apartment, but I stood beside my mother. Dad was on the other side of her, a tall statue, uncomfortable in his blue suit coat on a hot day that wasn't even Sunday. His hands were clasped in front of him, calloused farmer hands, still now, rather than grasping the wheel of his combine.

They walked in slowly, and I was aware of every eye on us. The church was full; there were rustlings and snifflings behind me, and I slumped beside my mother, a part of the Pearson clan we both were now, a terrible page in the picture book.

The Pearsons sat stoically on the hard wooden pews, staring tragically ahead, blue eyes rimmed with a burning red. Ole was different. He slid down in his seat and lay his head against his sister Alice's, shoulder. I knew nothing of what the preacher said. I only knew that Mrs. Bain had played "Savior, like a Shepherd, Lead Us" on the tinny piano as we had marched in. It might haunt me forever. I knew it would.

We drove in a procession to the graveyard, and Dad parked the car on a side road. Others were already there, plodding across the dried grass to the gravesite. I hadn't seen a graveyard before, with its headstones sticking up ominously, announcing to all that death was certain. I didn't like it.

"You stay here, Janie." My mother said, as I put my hand to the car door handle. "We won't be gone long."

I felt a relief at that, and yet I wanted to go, too, to see it through to the end. But Mom had whispered no, and she shook her head slightly, as she shut her car door, and followed Dad toward the terrible place in the middle of the graveyard.

It was somehow for my protection. My mother's eyes had said so. Protection from some awful truth that I knew already.

I stared out the other window of the car, away from the graveyard. A wheat field grew all the way to the edge of the two-rut road. Wind tossed the ripened grain, and its familiar rustle was like a warm song, touching the ice inside me. It seemed like Ray wasn't gone—he wasn't over there by that grave. He was here, all around me. I could almost see him parting the grain, and trudging out of that wheat field, onto the rutted road, and up to my car window. He would smile and tap on the window and ask, "What's everybody *here* for?"

A gravelly footstep close by startled me, and I looked around to see the funeral director's son shuffling along the road. He was dressed up fancy, helping his dad in this chilling business, but he was only a few years older than I was. He saw me in the car, and smiled, a sad little smile.

It was the same smile I had imagined was Ray's. But it was not Ray—it could never be Ray. Suddenly the tears trapped inside me were free, gushing from my eyes as if burst from a dam. I wiped them furiously but more kept coming, so I ducked down in the seat where the boy wouldn't see me, and hid there until Mom and Dad came back, and the tears were dried on my face.

People had brought food to the house—steaming casseroles, chocolate cakes with nut-studded frosting, potato salads. The Birthday Club ladies were there, I saw them, placing their offerings of food on the long table, then sitting in the kitchen with the others, on hard, straight-backed chairs with paint peeling at the edges.

Nobody said much. It was quiet for so many people to be sitting there, mostly staring with dreary eyes, and picking at their clothes. Dad had disappeared into a bedroom and shut the door. Mom whispered to me to get her a comb and brush. Then she set me down on a stool and began combing out my hair. "It's a mess," she whispered to me. "What did you do?"

I shrugged. Something in her could not stand messy hair, even at a time like this. Or perhaps she just needed to do something with her hands, anything. I leaned back against my mother's round stomach, as my hair was quickly turned into French braids. I could feel the baby's soft kicks against my head. A life had ended—way too soon. But now another was beginning. And these people in the kitchen would watch this baby grow, with love and acceptance, because this baby belonged here.

I slipped from the stool, from the sorrowful eyes in the room, from the choking silence. I left by the back door, letting it close softly, and dropped down on the steps.

Cubby was there. He saw me, crawled up beside me, and dropped his black head onto my lap. His brown eyes quivered as he looked up at me. I laid my hand on his head, then hugged him close so I could feel the sigh in his throat and his dog breath on my cheek. He was mine, now. No one had to say it. It was something Cubby and I just knew.

It was an animal knowledge, strong as a sinew, a gut thread beginning to sew my picture into this book, this

Place of Belonging. It almost seemed the thread was getting tighter now, as though to keep my heart here forever, beating in some secret frog place, and never leaving at all.

CHAPTER FIFTEEN

ANOTHER BABY

SEPTEMBER WAS LONG, and I awoke to the bird's songs, just like always—those happy twitterings and meadowlark calls, just as if everything was fine and happy, but it wasn't. The days were hot, with cool around the edges when the sun faded beneath the Rockies. The harvest was over now, the hard work done, and only the pain remained. But Ray had been right. Life goes on, and we all did, Dad hiding his grief in his cup of coffee, and never mentioning Ray again, not that I heard, though his grief was like a heavy, silent cloud that hovered, without words.

It was in the evening, after a hard day of laundry and cleaning and cooking that Mom sank into the yellow kitchen chair. Grandma was there, up to her elbows in bubbly dish water. She turned around. "What's wrong?" she asked, and her dark eyes said she knew what was wrong, and she didn't like it.

My mother breathed out a long flow of air. "I think I'm in labor," she said. "I've been kind of feeling like it all day."

"Oh, for goodness' sakes!" Grandma grabbed a dish towel and dried her hands. "Where's Gunder? You're going to town right now!"

Mom laughed. "It's not that bad yet," she said. "I have plenty of time. I'll go in tomorrow."

I came around the corner then, carrying Nancy, with Johnny close behind. "Where are you going tomorrow?" I asked.

My mother leaned forward and lifted Nancy from my arms. "Well, guess what," she said. "James is going to be born. Maybe tomorrow."

I smiled and squeezed Johnny's hand. James was the name they had chosen for this baby, who was sure to be a boy. We won't call him Jimmy, either, or Jim, Mom had explained. Just James. It was a worthy name. And now he was going to be born! I could hardly wait.

Grandma came around the corner of the kitchen then, lugging my mother's suitcase that had been packed for days.

"What are you doing with that?" Mom asked.

"You're going to town, Harriet," Grandma said. "Straight to the hospital." There was no going to Great Falls this time. Conrad was their hometown now, and this baby would be born there, in that hospital on the tree-lined street just blocks from Grandma's apartment. And my mother was going there, immediately.

"Oh, I don't think so," Mom said. "I told you it's not that bad yet."

"I heard Dad's truck down by the granary," My voice was high-pitched and hopeful. "He'll be in for coffee pretty soon, I'll bet."

"Of course he will," Grandma said. "And when he comes in that door, you're going straight to town."

My mother smiled and shook her head. "No," she said. "And I don't know why you're having such a fit about it. I'll go when I think it's time."

"If you don't get to town, then I'm leaving," Grandma said. "I can't stand being here and you having that baby right here in the house with no doctor and maybe something going wrong. Gunder will have to take me in or else I'll walk."

I looked at Grandma's face, brown eyes narrowed and threatening, worry lines deepening in her forehead. She had already lost two daughters young, I knew, one from a pregnancy gone wrong. Dark-haired Aunt Ruby had died at age twenty-two, and beautiful Aunt Maibelle, with her silken hair and hazel eyes, had died at age thirty-four, expecting her fourth baby, but not living to give birth. Now my mother was her only daughter left. The two women stared at each other, Mom's usual smile faded and gone. I knew a stand-off when I saw one, and this was a big one. Grandma would walk to town, all fifteen miles, and everyone knew it. She would plod along the side of the road, kicking through the weedy edges, maybe stumbling, maybe falling, but getting up and shoving one foot after the other. All fifteen miles.

My mother sighed. "All right," she said, then her face tightened as another contraction swept through her stomach. "This is so dumb, but *all right.*"

And when Dad came in the door for coffee, Grandma was waiting and shoved the suitcase into his surprised hand. "No time to lose," was all she said, and she stood there waiting while they looked at each other and my mother shrugged. Then they were in the car and driving away down the long graveled road, a little poof of dust kicking up behind them.

Grandma walked to the yellow chair and plopped into it, wiping her forehead with the white hankie she always seemed to have. "I'll get some supper for us pretty quick," she said to me. "Then we'll get the kids ready for bed and go there ourselves soon as dishes are done."

I made a face, but not so Grandma could see. It didn't sound like a fun evening. But maybe it was for the best. Who knew what tomorrow would bring? I lingered for a while beside the little pink crib that was for new babies. It had been painted blue for Johnny, then pink for Nancy. Now it was all ready to embrace a new baby—yellow blankets folded neatly, and the crib sheet with clowns stretched tight against the small mattress. I hoped that James wouldn't mind a pink crib. I'd explain it all to him someday, how everybody was too busy and too sad to paint it blue again. He'd understand.

I awoke the next morning with the sound of pans being shoved under the cupboard and clanging against each other. Grandma never did try to be quiet when she was making breakfast. If she had pancakes going, then you'd better get up and eat them, no matter how early it was. I heard Nancy banging a spoon on the high chair tray, and Johnny's high voice asking for a drink. Then Dad's low voice saying he'd have more coffee, please.

I sat straight up in bed, and grabbed for my clothes on the floor beside me. James must have been born or Dad would still be in town. I dressed and ran around the corner of the living room to the kitchen.

"How's James?" I asked, looking straight at Dad.

He grinned. "It's a girl," he said. "Seven pounds, ten ounces. Real pretty, too."

Grandma slapped another pancake onto his plate. "That's why I always said you shouldn't name a baby 'fore it's born," she said.

I leaned against the door frame, the picture of James in my mind suddenly changing into a whole different baby, one I hadn't had time to imagine right. "What's her name, then?" I asked.

"Judith Anne," Dad said. "Anne for Grandma." He nodded in Grandma's direction. Grandma's name, which nobody actually called her, was Maude Anne. So this was perfect. Grandma seemed pleased, too, smiling into the pancake batter.

"Judy Anne," I whispered, to see how it would sound.

Dad heard me. "Your mother says she wants to call her Judith," he said. "Not Judy. Just Judith."

It was like James, then. Not Jim or Jimmy. Just James. Just Judith.

But Judith became Judy the second day after she was home from the hospital. My mother even said it first. "I'm so glad we didn't paint the crib blue," she said. "It needed to stay pink for Judy."

And I was proud because I could pick this baby right up from that crib and not have to wait until someone placed her carefully in my arms. I was getting that old now, old enough to take care of a baby all by myself, almost.

Judy was a quiet baby, smiling easily, and hardly fussing at all. "This is a sweet baby," my mother said one day. "A real sweet one." I nodded my agreement. "And it's a good thing Grandma made me go in when I did," she said. "This baby came out real easy. I almost had her in the elevator at the hospital. I could have had her at home, no trouble at all. Probably should have."

But I had slid down the wall and sat on the floor, just at the thought. It was what Grandma had been afraid of, I knew. Sometimes it just paid to get stubborn and say you're gonna walk to town. Otherwise, who knew what could happen, if something went wrong and there you were. Grandma was right again, just like always.

Judy had soft dark hair, and I held my pigtail close to the baby's head to see if it was the same shade of brown. It almost was. I thought it would be nice, now, to have a baby sister with brown hair like mine. But then, before I even knew it, the dark hair was replaced by strands of blonde—white blonde that blazed in the sun and got whiter by the day. It was no use. I would always be the different one, with my dark hair and eyes, and everyone would know, could tell it by looking.

"I guess these babies don't look like us," my mother said one day, her hand on my shoulder. "With all that blonde hair."

"And blue eyes," I said.

"But we like it, don't we." My mother was proud of those babies, who all looked like little Swedes. And I agreed. They were beautiful, no doubt about it. Anybody'd be proud of those babies.

CHAPTER SIXTEEN

ACCORDION LESSONS

MOM AND DAD WERE PLANNING A TRIP—a long trip in the car, clear across Montana and North Dakota, into Minnesota and the town of Bemidji. All three babies were going, and Grandma, too, as far as Uncle Kenny's in North Dakota.

"We'll be gone about ten days," my mother said to me. "And I've made arrangements for you to stay with Miss Walker across the road. That way you won't miss any school."

I just stared out the window. I liked Miss Walker, I truly did—but ten days?

"Honey, you wouldn't like to go on this trip, anyway. We're just going to visit some old people, and you wouldn't find that interesting."

I glanced back at my mother. I would find it interesting. Of course I would. "What old people?" I asked.

"Dad's uncle and some others, I don't know who all, but relatives of his that he hasn't seen in ages and he thinks it's time. And besides, you'll need to get the mail and take care of Cubby and the cats."

I smiled at this, because I knew I'd let Cubby and the cats come in the house every day, just for a little while. It wouldn't be so bad, this staying with Miss Walker.

Miss Walker seemed glad to have the company, too. She fixed fancy little dinners for the two of us, with silver-rimmed china and flowered tea-cups. She was trying new recipes, I knew, like a practice for some husband that wasn't found yet, some bachelor farmer, grizzled and hardened by the soil, drinking coffee from a mug.

I walked back across the road one day after feeding Cubby and the swarm of cats on the back step. Strange sounds were coming from the tiny house where Miss Walker lived and waited. (She *was* waiting for something, I knew. Something better than she had.) Now a discord of notes like a strangled organ was escaping out the framework of the house.

I opened the door, and there Miss Walker sat, a large music box on her lap. It looked like a little piano on one side, and a row of buttons on the other. "What *is* it?" I asked.

"It's an accordion," Miss Walker said in her school-teacher

voice. "I've had it a long time, but I can't play it. Used to belong to my mother, but she couldn't play it, either. You take piano lessons. Here. You try it."

Miss Walker slipped the black straps from her shoulders, and stood up, with the heavy thing moaning in a minor key. I sat down and Miss Walker placed it on my skinny legs and draped the straps around my shoulders.

I did take piano lessons, had for two years now, practicing when the kids were napping, because that's the only time I could. "Soft-pedal it," my mother would say, "So they don't wake up." How they could even sleep through it, I didn't know, but if they woke up, my practicing was over, and I was secretly glad. But still Mrs. Bain, my piano teacher, thought I did good, thought I practiced a lot. No need to tell her different, either.

But this was no piano. It seemed to have a soul all its own, yearning to open its folded bellows and blare into the sky. I could play a song in the key of C—Twinkle, Twinkle Little Star. And if I pressed the studded button with my left hand, it matched, then one up or down for G or F. It was starting to get easy. It was fun. The accordion liked me, responding to my songs, one after the other.

"There. Now see? I knew you could play it," Miss Walker said, as if I had suddenly solved an arithmetic problem. And that was hardly likely. "And you can play this whenever you like. See, that's where I keep it." She pointed to a darkened space under her bed. "I sleep on it all night." It was like an exquisite secret. I looked at my teacher. Miss Walker would rather have a husband, I knew, but I didn't say a word about that.

I played the accordion so much that the ten days just melted into a fog of squalling notes, and when Mom and Dad came home, I was almost sad to leave Miss Walker, and felt sorry for her, living alone like that.

My mother was glad to be home, and she sat down with Judy on the edge of her bed, fingering the yellow chenille bedspread. I sat beside her, trying to imagine in my head the long straight road across Montana that she was describing, the fields and sloughs of North Dakota and the wooded lakes of Minnesota. "One thing you would have liked," she said. "A statue of Paul Bunyan and his blue ox, Babe, there in Bemidji. We took pictures, and you can see it when we get them developed."

I just listened on. "And then—oh I have to tell you this—" she tilted her head back and laughed, a giggly, girlish laugh that made me laugh, too, but I didn't know what was funny yet. "Gunder's uncle's wife just loved holding Judy. She couldn't see very well, but she would stroke her blond hair. When she asked me what the baby's name was, I said 'Judith.' And she replied in her strong Swedish accent, 'Oh yah. Yoodit. T'at's a good Svedish name. Yoodit." And my mother laughed again. I knew she was proud of this, funny as it was. A good Swedish name was a fine thing to have.

"Mom," I said, reeling in my thoughts of a Swedish lady saying "Yoodit." "Mom, Miss Walker has an accordion."

"Oh?" she said as she reached for a diaper. The baby needed changing. "That's nice."

"And I can play it," I said. "Miss Walker said I can play it whenever I want."

"That's so nice of her," my mother said. "We're very lucky to have her here as a teacher, don't you think?"

"Well, I can play hymns on it," I said. "I practiced Amazing Grace for two days straight."

Mom fastened the last pin on the diaper, and I reached for the baby, and held her tightly against my chest. "Miss Walker says I can play it pretty good, and I don't even know how."

My mother looked at me now, new interest in her dark eyes. "Well, when Dad's done with work tonight, we'll have to borrow Miss Walker's accordion and you can play it for us."

And that's how I came to be struggling with the black accordion case, hoisting it into Johnny's red wagon, and pulling it across the road, as the sun was flashing its last pink strips across the sky. "I'll bring it right back," I had told Miss Walker. "And I'll be real careful with it."

"I know you will," Miss Walker said. "My mother would have been glad to know you could play it. It's sort of for her, Janie."

And I touched the accordion case almost reverently, and hoped I could play it good enough for Miss Walker's mother.

They sat in a circle, Dad, Mom holding Judy, then Johnny and Nancy in little chairs. Even Grandma dragged in a chair and sat reluctantly in it. "Don't like accordions," she said. "Never did. Too loud."

And I knew it would be loud, and there was nothing I could do about that. Amazing Grace roared from the bellows and filled the room with groans and sobs, all in the key of G.

"That was quite good," my mother announced, while Grandma said nothing.

"Yah," Dad said. "She could play that when we do our visitation."

And then I shut the accordion up tight and put it away as fast as I could. I didn't want to play it for visitation. Not ever. I was much too shy for anything like that.

"She probably could," Mom said. "They'd probably like that."

"Don't think they would," Grandma said, as she got up from her chair, but no one paid attention.

Dad's "visitation" was on Sunday afternoons when he visited old people who lived alone. "Need anything?" he'd ask, and if they did, he'd get it. Then he'd have a word of prayer, and go on to the next old person's house. I had gone with him twice, but lately I'd stayed with the kids so Mom could go along. The kids were too active for the old people. But the accordion? Dad seemed to think it would be fine, not too loud or squawky, at all. I had visions of my lazy Sunday afternoons swirling away forever in a haze of old people and accordions.

For a while, that's what I did on Sunday afternoons. "That's Lenore Ellingson's place," Dad said, as he drove up in front of a little white house with tiny windows and a tacked-on porch. "They used to farm west of Ledger there, years ago."

And the lady with the faded blue eyes and skin like shriveled parchment smiled at me as I played Amazing Grace and even sang along in her high, quivering voice. Later, after the word of prayer, she tried to help put the accordion in its case, folding down one of the straps so I could close it. "I used to play when I was a girl," she said, her voice sounding like an echo from another day. "Not this, of course, but I could play the piano." She reached for a chair and sat down. "But that was a long time ago."

Then we were at the next house. Don Buford lived there, with his second wife, Thelma. "First wife died in a tractor accident," Dad said. "They used to farm north of Ledger."

I wondered if everyone in Conrad used to farm near Ledger, and now they all lived in little houses and apartments around town, with their closed up rooms too hot and smelling of stale bacon and their eyes too clouded to see. Sometimes Dad would have to talk loud, almost shout, "NEED ANYTHING?" so they could hear him. But they all heard Amazing Grace on the accordion, and they could sing along, too, if they liked.

The Sunday afternoon we drove to see Sam and Carrie Sollid was a day warmed by sunshine that sparkled on the trees and beamed down onto the car roof, right into my soul. It made me want to run through a pasture or maybe climb up into the hayloft, flop across a fragrant, musty straw bale and read. Just read, while the barn cats flicked their tails across my face. But here we were in the car, rattling up a dusty road, while the kids whined, and Miss Walker's accordion slid around in the trunk. I wished we didn't have it along. Sam and Carrie Sollid were not shut-ins. They were old, all right, but not shut-ins. They had lived in Conrad as long as anyone could recall. Sam knew everybody, or so it was told, and his word was well-respected around town.

"I have to give Sam these papers from Bernhard," Dad had said to Mom in the front seat. "Thought they might like to hear Janie play Amazing Grace."

The last time I had seen Sam and Carrie was when I went with my mother to pick crab apples from Sam's little orchard. He had hauled out a ladder and was helping gather the crab apples, dropping them with tiny pings into the tin bucket. "These make wonderful jelly," Carrie had said, in her high smooth voice which sounded somehow out of place in her worn face. "It should turn out fine for you."

"I'm sure it will," Mom said. "I got your recipe right here." She touched her pocket. "I'll bring you back some."

"Don't you do it," Sam's voice growled from the next tree over. "Carrie made five hundred thousand pints and I gotta eat it all."

"As if you couldn't," Carrie said, still smiling.

And now we were driving up to Sam and Carrie's farm, and I would be lugging in the accordion, right through the kitchen, past the rows of crab apple jelly on the shelves, right to the living room to play Amazing Grace.

And when I had finished and the last gasp of air had hissed from the bellows, Sam looked over at Dad. "She can play it all right," he said, "but if she had a few lessons she could learn to play the dang thing pretty good." It was as if I wasn't there. "You know Irene Carlbom?"

Dad nodded. He knew everybody, too. "Still lives with her folks there on Third?"

"Yep," Sam said. "She gives accordion lessons, has for some time now."

Dad seemed to be thinking about this, his blue eyes staring at Sam, but he said nothing.

"And another thing." Sam wasn't finished. "That accordion's too big for her. Look at it. It was made for a big man. They make smaller ones for ladies. I saw a woman playin' one at a dance hall in Great Falls. Don't know where she got it."

I had silently slipped Miss Walker's accordion from my shoulders, and dropped it into its case with a quiet thud. Sam was right. The accordion hung like a wash machine from my shoulders. But a smaller one? I shook my head, even though the men were now talking about wheat. Might as well wish for the moon. I was lucky to have Miss Walker's to play, but Sam didn't know that.

Irene Carlbom gave accordion lessons from the porch of her parent's home. It was boarded up and windowed, just like a room, but you could tell it used to be a porch, with hooks for the swing still stuck wistfully in the ceiling and the wooden floor tinged with peeling green paint. But it quickly became a music studio when Irene Carlbom stepped in.

Now I took two lessons a week, both on Tuesday. First the piano lesson at Mrs. Bain's, and then to Irene Carlbom's. I learned to shove the bellows right, back and forth, and to play little runs on the bass to hold the melody together.

It wasn't hard to figure out that the piano was for classical music, serious and intense, music that thundered through your brain and made you sit still and listen. The accordion was for dancing, for laughter, for singing along. I didn't know which I liked best. But one thing was sure. I could take the accordion down by the barn to practice and it wouldn't wake up the kids, or bother Grandma. It could be as loud as it wanted, and it wanted to be plenty loud. Even Cubby would creep away, his tail hanging low, when he saw the accordion.

CHAPTER SEVENTEEN

DOG DAYS FOR SNAKES

I WASN'T SURPRISED WHEN MY MOTHER made her announcement one spring morning. Another winter had passed, and the men were in the fields again, with planting and summer fallowing. I had suspected it, with all the gagging and running to the outhouse to vomit. And Judy was getting bigger now, and could stand alone, though she was only nine months old. Another baby was on the way, was due around the first of December, around Dad's birthday.

He was pleased with this, especially, I could tell, though he didn't spend a lot of time with the babies when they were tiny, or carry them much. He waited until they were older and could walk by themselves. Then he would reach down and lift them high to his face, kiss them, and carry them around the house. I always watched this from the side of the room, by the corner, or from the yellow kitchen chair. I did not know how it felt to be lifted in a strong man's arms, because I was seven before I even saw him. Much too old to be carried, legs hanging down. The thought made me laugh, it seemed so funny. A laugh that stretched over a pit somewhere inside me, stretched tight so as not to loose a terrible longing that wanted to escape.

But now I was busy with Judy, trying to teach her to walk. I shoved the yellow chair out of the corner and stood Judy there, wobbly on her legs, but standing alone. Then I would hold out my hands, one inch away, and Judy would stumble into my arms, until she could finally take one step, then two, all by herself.

"Honey, she's only a baby," my mother would say on her way by with a load of diapers.

"Johnny walked this young," I said. "And Nancy younger than that."

"I know." Mom sighed, then hurried past.

Grandma looked on with approval. "Time to get them off the dirty floor," she said. As if any floor could be dirty with Grandma around, with her constant sweeping and mopping. When Grandma wasn't there, though, my mother didn't care that much about the floors. If Judy picked up some unknown glob from the floor and put it in her mouth, Mom would simply say, "Oh ish," and probe around in the baby's mouth with her deft fingers that had practice rolling up curlers for permanent waves.

I felt that this might be the last summer for me to be a child myself, perhaps. The number thirteen was looming up in October. Thirteen years old. Time to be a woman, almost. I knew I couldn't act like it, though. It didn't feel right, not yet. I still wanted to climb in the barn and run to the pasture for the cow.

I had invented a new game and had shown Margaret how it was done. It was called Walking Around the Farm Without Touching the Ground. It started in the trees by the house, where fallen logs stretched across the side of the grove until some piles of lumber appeared, which you scampered across, to the corral fence by the cattle shed. It went on for some distance, circling the granaries until you came to the hay bales. Easy to get across those, then balance on the fence by the barn until you came to the old garage and you were done. If at any time, you fell off something and hit the ground, you had to start over. It could go on for hours, if you had hours, which I didn't. So far I had only reached the cattle shed without falling, a little farther than Margaret, who had only reached the chicken coop.

It was September now, and the harvest wasn't quite finished. School had started and Judy's birthday was two weeks away, her first. My mother liked to have a special celebration for the first birthday, and was already planning it. And I had taken Johnny and Nancy outside on this Saturday morning, the sun baking down on the dried grasses and the sky solid blue to the mountains.

I tried to teach them my game, but they were too young. Johnny could make it to the end of the first log, but Nancy always fell off, right about the middle.

"Tell you what," I said. "Wait for me at the cattle shed. I always make it that far." And Johnny walked off with his balancing stick, Nancy following behind, her dolly wrapped in her arms with its white blanket trailing in the dust.

I hurried. I fell off twice and started over. Then I decided to get back up and keep going, even if I fell. The kids were at the cattle shed by the time I reached the corral fence. They'd gone inside the empty shed and were setting up a playhouse on some old rusted machinery, the floor a carpet of dried cow dung.

I balanced on top of the corral, Cubby leaping mindlessly on the outside of the fence. I glanced down at him, and he yipped up at me like he wanted me to jump down. I shook my head at him as though he could understand. And then I lost my balance and felt myself falling on the opposite side, where some waist-high weeds crept along the inside of the corral fence.

I landed on my feet, then felt it. Two metal prongs like fire, like lightening, struck at my leg, just above my foot. My whole leg was on fire, starting from those tiny pricks. *What was it?*

I hopped out of the weeds on one foot, and ran toward the children. I glanced down at my ankle, and saw that red streaks were racing up my leg, out of sight under the rolled-up jeans. I bent down and looked, Cubby by this time pressing against me, panting and licking my face. I could see two punctures an inch apart and below them two small needle-like holes. Four in all. Now a purple streak, like a bruise, sprang from the larger punctures and joined the red streaks spreading up my leg.

I felt cold, and in an instant time froze, like an eternity in a moment. I hadn't heard a rattle, hadn't heard anything, after all those times of running from grasshopper whirrs. I hadn't seen a snake in those weeds. But the serpent's mark was on my leg, a mouth with fangs an inch apart had struck me there, sure as anything.

The kids. Cubby and I had to get them out of there, now. Back to the house. Back to where Mom hummed in the kitchen and the little battery clock radio played softly on the counter. Back to Life.

We started back, with me telling the kids to run, but I walked slowly, Cubby beside me. I had heard that you shouldn't run if ever you got bit by a rattlesnake, that running only made the poison go faster. Poison. I glanced up at the sky. It was so shrilly blue.

I wanted to live. And I wasn't sure what would happen. Dad didn't go to doctors, hardly ever, everybody knew that. And I hadn't seen a snake, or heard it rattle. What if it was just a hunk of barbed wire in those weeds? I hadn't even gone back to look. So they might not think it was a snake bite, but I knew it was. There are things you just know somehow, like a clock inside you ringing an alarm that only you can hear.

Dad was in the kitchen, having his morning coffee break, hot rolls and doughnuts scattered across the table. Mom looked at my leg first, and frowned. "You didn't see anything?" she asked, and I said no. There was a silence. I hadn't seen a snake or heard it rattle. There were only the puncture marks and the vicious red and blue streaks. Dad was still harvesting, shouldn't have even been in for coffee. The silence grew longer, the moments ticking away from the clock on the counter.

Then Dad screeched his chair back and stood to his feet. "Get the kids in the car," he said to Mom, and was out the door. I sat in the back seat and stretched my leg as far as I could. I glanced out the window at the fields rushing and rattling past on both sides of the graveled road. Dust stood out behind us like a thunderous cloud.

"Gunder, not so fast." Mom's voice was tense, but Dad didn't reply. Just kept driving until we reached the highway, then he taxied down the two lane runway and aimed for the sky. The world flew by on both sides of the car. Maybe I wouldn't die from a snake bite. Maybe we would all die in this car. The blue of the sky rushed in and out between the trees and the telegraph wires. I stared at it until I could hardly see. God was out there somewhere. "Please, Lord, help us." My voice was just a squeak, hardly anything at all, but He must have heard me, for the car was slowing. Conrad's quiet, familiar streets were gliding past. Now the hospital loomed, brown and official, like it alone could save the world. The car jerked to a stop, dust swirling around it. We were still alive.

Doctor Hadcock appeared in the small emergency room, his white lab coat askew, and his stethoscope dangling from his neck. "Let's see this," he said and he bent over my leg as I stretched on the narrow table. His glasses were thick, making his eyes large and round, like an owl's. He looked at the puncture marks and the red streaks, turning my leg so he could see better. Without warning, he shoved a needle into my leg near the puncture wounds, making another that hurt just as bad, though he said it was to deaden the pain. Beulah, his nurse, was peering over his shoulder. Then, as if on cue from a prompter behind a curtain, I saw her hand the doctor a small wicked knife and a devise with a plastic hose attached to it.

"You sure you didn't see a snake or hear a rattle?" he asked once more, though we had told him that before. I nodded.

"Well, this appears to be a snake bite," he said. "We have to assume it was a rattler. Good thing you came right in."

His fingers moved quickly over the fang marks, and without another word, he drew a cross over the place with the small knife. I could feel it cut deeply, though I sensed no pain. My eyes were scrunched tightly shut. I felt the hose devise clamp down, and a vacuum-like sense of blood being pulled from my leg.

"Ooooh," Beulah said, and I wondered why, but I didn't look. Already I felt faint, my head twirling around somewhere above me.

"It doesn't surprise me that she didn't hear anything," Doctor Hadcock said to my mother, who was sitting nearby, trying not to watch. "This time of year, a rattlesnake will shed its skin and sometimes won't rattle before it strikes. Sometimes they can't even see and she might have jumped down real close to it or even on it, and it just struck. Yep," he said, and he finished sticking the last bit of tape to the bandage around my leg. "It's dog days for rattlesnakes."

I opened my eyes at that and looked straight at my mother's face. This sounded really funny, and Mom's eyes twinkled. We would laugh at this when we got home, I knew it. Dog days for snakes. What about elephant days for chickens? Cow days for cats? I smiled as I sat up, this time trying not to look at my mother, so she wouldn't laugh right now.

Doctor Hadcock was still talking and he was serious. He said Dog Days for Snakes twice more, before he was finished. "We've given her horse serum," he said finally, "and she'll need to stay here overnight. But she can be checked out of the hospital tomorrow, if she can stay in town for a few days."

Well, of course I could. With Grandma. And Grandma hovered over me, bringing me tea and slices of nutty banana bread, fresh brownies, huge glasses of milk. It was as if I were a child again, just Grandma and me, rummaging through Grandma's ancient pictures, asking who those stark people from another age were, reading worn books while Grandma did crossword puzzles, listening to the little radio at night, a football game between the Conrad Cowboys and the Shelby Coyotes, while Grandma finished up the supper dishes in her small sink, then handed me a piece of rhubarb pie for dessert. It was almost worth it, getting bit by that snake.

CHAPTER EIGHTEEN

A BIRTHDAY GIFT

Miss Walker was leaving. She had explained it all to me as if we were best friends, as if only I could understand. She had received a marriage proposal from an old farmer friend near Billings, a man the age of her father, whose wife had died two years ago. "Now he isn't any Prince Charming," she'd said, like she was talking about geography. "But I've known him a long time, and he's nice and kind, and could you ask for more?" Well, yes, I thought, but didn't say it.

Some people were mad at Miss Walker for leaving like this, and she felt it. "But I *have* to," she said to me, her voice sounding ragged and frantic. "If I postpone this, or make him wait a year, it'll be too late. There are plenty of other women around there to snatch him up in a second." I nodded in agreement, like I was wise and knew it to be true. I swallowed my doubts like a wad of old chewing gum. This was what Miss Walker wanted more than anything, her brass ring on the carousel. If it came around, she had to grab it, no matter how it seemed to anybody else.

Her small table and chairs, the rickety bed, the precious box of fancy china, were all packed in the bed of a farm truck, bound by bristly strands of rope. She'd said a tearful good-bye, and took the heavy black accordion case from my hand. It went up on the truck, too, set mournfully between two tipped-over chairs. I watched them drive away, disappearing over the first rise. The only thing left of Miss Walker was a choking cloud of dust whirling there, like it had swallowed her alive.

Mrs. Campbell, the county school superintendent had driven out, a squat lady with a purple suit and glasses that hung on her nose. "I've got a teacher coming," she assured Dad, who was the school board chairman. "He's from New York, he and his wife, Joe and Connie Petura. Seemed rather eager to try life in Montana."

I had never seen anyone from New York. I waited patiently for their arrival, while the school missed a whole week of lessons. New furniture from Arnot's in Conrad was delivered, a white table and matching chairs, much nicer than Miss Walker's had been. A new bed, too, better than any the Pearsons had. They must have money, these people from New York.

They drove up on a shimmering Saturday afternoon, their car a late model Plymouth which would have been fine, but it was red, and already seemed out of place as it rolled up next to the plain little school, and carefully stopped.

Joe and Connie Petura stepped out and the welcoming committee of the Pearsons and the Moores crowded around to shake their hands. Joe stepped out first, a thin, dark-haired man with glasses and breath that smelled like stale pipe tobacco. He shook everyone's hands and said hello in a nasally voice that sounded different, a way of talking that I didn't recognize. But I was busy looking at Connie, who had crawled out of the car after Joe, and stood apart from him, staring at us with cat-like eyes, disinterest turning to hate right before us. I could feel it. Connie hated us all, even Joe. She turned her cold face to her husband. "I'm going inside." Her voice was nasally, too, like his. She stomped toward the small house waiting nearby, it's door timidly hanging half-open, as if afraid to welcome this angry woman. Margaret and I looked at each other, eyes wide.

Joe Petura seemed embarrassed and after a few more attempts to say something nice, especially to Mrs. Campbell, he hurried into the house after Connie. Before any of us had left the yard, a few shouts were heard, coming from the kitchen. Connie's voice exploded, calling Joe a name I had never heard before.

Mrs. Campbell shook her head. "It's too bad," she whispered, as if to excuse the whole thing. "Had to take whoever I could get on this short notice. I'm sure Mr. Petura will be a fine teacher. He's very qualified."

Then she was gone in her car, to some important meeting in Conrad, and we were left with the people from New York, who were in their house, Joe's voice now added to the shouting. I was shocked. Didn't they like their white table and chairs and fancy bed? Couldn't they look out the window and see the Rockies there on the horizon, shining in the sun? Didn't they know this was a really nice day?

Mr. Petura was, in fact, a fine teacher, especially in English, which was my favorite subject. He didn't do so well in arithmetic, his explanations never as good as Miss Walker's had been. But he tried.

Connie, though, was not trying. I could see her from the schoolhouse window, sitting at her white table, playing solitaire. She slapped the cards down like she was killing flies, her hands quick and murderous. She never said hello to the school kids, tried not to look at them at all, just played her solitaire, hour by hour, day by day, stopping only to yell at Joe when he ventured near.

"She's probably very lonely and misses her old home," Mom said to me one morning. "We need to reach out to her and show her that people in Montana are friendly, Christian people. Don't you think so?"

I nodded, but I didn't agree. That wouldn't work. I'd tried that already, had said hello twice to Connie when I saw her outside. Connie had just made a snorting sound in her throat and pushed past on her way to the outhouse. I even rode my bike by the school late one afternoon, practicing my yodeling so Connie could hear and experience Montana in all its glory. I didn't yodel for just anyone. But even that failed to produce a response, at least a good one. Connie, strange as it may have been, didn't seem to like Montana at all.

Then, one day, Connie was gone. She'd called for a taxi in the middle of the night, called for one clear from Great Falls, sixty miles away. It was the talk of the neighborhood. "Lure of the bright lights," Dad had said, as if that explained everything. Nothing further to add. And if it bothered Joe

Petura at all, he didn't show it. I wondered if he cried at night, but how could you cry for Connie?

One morning just before recess, I stepped up to Mr. Petura's desk with my English assignment neatly finished. He had his back turned, coaching the first graders in spelling. I was about to place my paper on his desk when I glanced down and saw a page, filled with his large familiar handwriting. It was to the local priest, Father Murphy. In a flash, like a billboard sign, I saw his complaints spelled out, way too easy to read. Connie "didn't want to be here. She yelled and threw pots and pans at me. She refused to lie with me." I dropped my assignment like it was on fire, and it fluttered from my hands like a burning leaf, curled and ashy, and covered the dreadful words on that page.

Mr. Petura's back was still turned, and I crept back to my desk and reached for my arithmetic book, opening to a page I didn't know, and read it mindlessly, like it was interesting. I wished I'd never seen that paper, wished I didn't read so fast and always read everything. All I could think of now was Connie. Poor, poor thing. I felt an overwhelming sympathy for her, even with all her yelling and solitaire and cold eyes, a sympathy that seeped out from me and followed Connie wherever she was, embracing her silently.

The next week Mr. Petura announced to the school that he and Connie were getting a divorce. "Don't worry about me leaving, though," he said. "I'll be here for a long time." Then he went back to Margaret's history lesson, like it was all that was on his mind. I knew better, though, knew that he would be leaving the second school was out in May, that he was already planning it in his mind, while he talked about Christopher Columbus. The way he looked out the window told me so. Like he was yearning for those bright lights, too, but the mountains were in the way.

I noted on the calendar that I would be thirteen on Friday the thirteenth of October. I told Margaret. "I think that might be bad luck," Margaret said. "Really bad luck, Janie." But I didn't care. I told everyone, like it was something special. My family wasn't superstitious, anyway, except for Grandma, who didn't like a black cat to cross her path. But Grandma didn't like any other kind of cat to cross her path, either.

"I've already had all the bad luck in the world," I told Margaret. "I jumped down on a rattlesnake, and my favorite teacher is gone with my accordion." I said *my* accordion, though it had never been, and Margaret knew that. I missed Miss Walker for sure, but the big accordion that clung to my skinny shoulders and bothered Grandma and scared Cubby, I missed that most of all.

"What kind of cake do you want for your birthday?" My mother asked me.

"Angel-food," I said, without a thought. The only kind of birthday cake Mom made was angel-food, though she always asked. It was my favorite, anyway, high and light, with lemony frosting dripping delicately down the sides.

Grandma was there the night of my birthday, and made scalloped corn while Mom fried the chicken. There was to be no every-day steak tonight. Fried chicken was for Sunday company or birthdays.

Even though it was my birthday, it had still been my job to catch the chicken, and I knew just the size—a young rooster, big enough to crow, but not too tough to eat. I had cornered one in the hay-shed, quickly grabbing its legs, while the wings flapped dust and feathers in my face. I was glad I didn't have to kill it. Grandma was here for that. Now it sizzled in the frying pan, while Mom finished mashing the potatoes.

My mother had placed thirteen candles on the cake and I had blown them out, every one. "And now." Her eyes were bright. "Gunder, get the present." He left the room, Johnny and Nancy racing after him, Judy toddling behind. I wondered why Dad was getting the present from another room, when it should be on the table by the cake, like always, my gifts of a new blouse, maybe a book, too. Some perfume.

Then he appeared around the corner, a heavy brown case in his hand. He set it in front of me and stood back. At first I couldn't open it, couldn't even try. I couldn't say anything, either. What if it wasn't what it looked like? How could it be that, anyway?

My fingers were shaking as I finally unlatched the case and lifted the lid. A shiny new accordion glistened there proudly, glistened with all its tight bellows and tiny buttons, its keys longing to be played. And across the front, set in silver letters was my name: *Janie Pearson*. Like a famous person's accordion, who played it on a stage while everyone danced. "Oh," was all I could say. "Oh." My voice was tiny and cracked, while the accordion suddenly swam in a blur of black and white and silver, but I dug it from its cocoon and draped it on. It was smaller. I could play it standing up. Amazing Grace was filling the room.

"Thank you, thank you," I said to everyone, over the music, while Johnny clapped his hands, and Nancy stomped up and down.

"It was your Dad's idea," Mom whispered to me later. "I wouldn't have thought we could get one, but he was in Great Falls one day, and went right to that dance hall Sam Sollid told him about, and you know he doesn't like dance halls, and asked about accordions. Somebody there told him where to get it, and he did, all by himself." Then she hugged me. "I knew you'd love it." But she didn't know the half.

CHAPTER NINETEEN

A NIGHT LIKE THIS

THE WIND WAS COLDER THAN USUAL that fall, raw and stinging, tossing tumbleweeds and dust across the farmyard. I couldn't take my new accordion down by the barn to practice now, so I used the bunkhouse. I practiced every day in there, while the wind beat the trees, their bare limbs scratching against the windows.

When Grandma was there, every Monday, the accordion hid under the bed. Dad had strung up wires in the bunkhouse west bedroom and clean, wet clothes, smelling of Oxydol, hung there to dry, the stove's warm vapors making the room like a steam bath. I slept out there with Grandma, sucking in the warm, moist air all around me while the clothes dried at night, and the accordion waited quietly under the bed.

Grandma liked the bunkhouse, particularly now, because the house was a mess and she couldn't fix it. They were putting in a bathroom, and had torn up the entry room where the men always washed their hands and hung their coats. "It's because of the electricity coming," Grandma said, "but it ain't here yet and who knows when it's gonna be. All this mess and no good cause."

I didn't answer because I knew Grandma was worried about something else, not the indoor bathroom, not the electricity. Another baby was coming, that was it, coming in December, due before Christmas. The worry wrinkles were getting deeper. And I just let Grandma mutter about the house. Best not to mention the baby right now, though I wanted to. Best to let Grandma talk about all the mess the men were making.

They had dug a big hole on the west side of the house for the septic tank, and called in some men from Conrad who knew how to do it, put in the tank and cover it up like a new grave. Bernhard came to help Dad turn the entry room into a real bathroom, tearing out old boards, nailing in new ones. George Moore helped paint, and Clint Rogers carefully laid down the new linoleum.

The entry window was spared, and became a bathroom window, complete with a lacy blue curtain. It seemed to take only a few days to me, but my mother thought it was taking too long. "Baby will be here before you know it," she said, rubbing her round belly. It would be much better having everything done by the time you came home with a new baby, especially in winter.

The men seemed to know this, too, and their pounding and painting became more intense, their jokes and laughter over coffee less frequent. By Thanksgiving, the house was ready for electricity, the bathroom finished. Mom said that was a lot to be thankful for. Their blessings were complete.

Dad would still have to haul the water, though, even with electricity, filling the cistern just like before. "We won't be able to use a lot of water," my mother explained to me. "No more than we ever have, just because it comes out of the faucet. Gotta remember that. Just a little for our baths." She drew an imaginary line on the side of the tub, way at the bottom. "But it will come out hot, when we want it." She smiled. "We won't have to heat the water on the stove."

And I wondered if I would miss the big tin bathtub hauled into the kitchen by the warm stove every Saturday night, the steamy water from a teakettle poured into it, pinging, splashing. I might miss that, just a little.

Judy's birth had been so easy that Mom was unprepared for this one. Dad had spent his birthday on December first, taking her in to the hospital, her labor already long and vicious. He brought Grandma out to the farm that evening, then drove straight back to town.

Grandma's forehead was pinched again, with those worry wrinkles. "Somethin's wrong," she said to me. "It's been a long time. The baby just can't come out."

I chewed on my lip, while Grandma paced. Back and forth before the kitchen sink, like it was a shrine and she was paying homage. Back and forth. I thought again of Grandma's other two daughters, my aunts, who had died so young. Back and forth Grandma marched, until she collapsed into the yellow chair, and folded her strong arms across her chest.

"Grandma, we just have to pray." I was whispering.

"That's what I'm doin.'" Grandma said. "Been prayin' for two days already."

Dad didn't come home that night, but he was at the farm by ten o'clock the next morning, his eyes bloodshot, his hair standing uncombed. "It's a boy," he said. "Daniel Raymond."

Then he smiled and his teeth gleamed white in his whiskered face. "Seven pounds, they said. Looks real healthy."

"How about Harriet?" Grandma asked. "I need to get to town to see her."

Dad nodded. "She's fine," he said. "A little tired. Baby wasn't born until early this morning. The doctor said the baby's head was large and was causing the problem. But he was finally born, and he looks fine to me."

I felt a long sigh escape from me, and I stepped over to Grandma and touched her hand. "Why don't you just go along into town and visit Mom," I said. "The kids and I'll be okay here until you get back. And tell me what the baby looks like." I suddenly felt that same excitement building inside me, the joy of a brand new baby. Who would he look like? When could I hold him? And thanks be to God, my mother was safe. She and that baby had struggled through the dark valley and emerged, alive, into the thin December sunlight.

Mom stayed in the hospital for eight days. "Used to keep them for two weeks," Grandma said. "Now they've cut it down to eight days. Hope she'll be okay. You have to help her a lot, Janie." And I nodded, knowing Grandma couldn't do everything, though she tried. We would both have to keep the laundry done, the kids fed, and the dishes washed, until Mom was on her feet once more.

It was snowing the day she came home, with Baby Daniel Raymond wrapped in a cocoon of blue. Dad opened the door and carried her suitcase in, and a tiny flurry of blizzard followed inside. Grandma got to hold the baby first, while Mom kissed the three children, climbing on her, especially lingering over Judy, who was still a baby, too, not even knowing the blue bundle was another one, smaller than herself.

Then Grandma gathered the children to the kitchen to feed them lunch, and I followed my mother to the bedroom. She had stories to tell of the long, intense labor, how the radio tune, "*Do the Hucklebuck*" twisted madly in her brain over and over, stabbing in and out between the spasms of labor. It wouldn't stop, and like the contractions, grew more desperate every minute. Then it was over. Baby Daniel Raymond opened his eyes and blinked at the harsh lights, waved a tiny arm.

"Come look at him, Janie," my mother said, pulling back the small flannel blanket. "So many folks came to visit and all the Pearsons said he looks like them." Her smile was sly, like she knew a secret. "But look at his eyes."

I crept closer, and rubbed my hand over the baby's head. He looked like a Pearson, as far as I could tell, blue eyes and all. Blond fuzz for hair. Like another beautiful Swedish baby.

"Look at those eyes," Mom said again. "They are wide-set eyes, like my Grandma Olson's were. I think he looks like my side, like an Olson. He may even look like my father someday, when he's a man. I'd bet on it, if I ever did that. And look here." She drew the blanket back further, under the baby's quivering chin. "Look at that dimple."

I looked closely, saw the dimple in his chin, and jumped back, stunned. "Where did he *get* it?" My voice was too loud, almost a shriek.

"From the same place you did, I suppose," my mother said. "Don't be so shocked. Remember the picture of my sister, Ruby?"

I nodded, the memory of the old photograph focusing in my brain, the dark haired girl standing in the snow, her shy smile, the deep dimple in her chin. Grandma had looked at the photo many times, caught her breath in a sigh, brushed her hand across it. "I remember," I said, my voice a whisper now.

"Well, Danny's dimple is just like Ruby's and just like yours."

And it was. At last. I could hold him, his face up to mine, and people could tell we looked alike if they saw our chins, with those dimples, just alike.

The baby was nursing now, and my mother was getting drowsy. I quietly left the room and ran for the bunkhouse. I dug my accordion from its hiding place under the bed, and began to play a song I hadn't heard before, a tune that I pulled from the air right through my soul. It was like a lullaby. So I made up words for it, about a baby boy with a dimple in his chin. I played it three more times so I wouldn't forget it and the last time I added more runs to the bass and ended it with the highest C the accordion had. It was ready.

Everyone was in the kitchen when I opened the door, dragging the accordion case after me. "Mom, I've made up a song for Danny, and I have to play it on the accordion. It's just for him."

"Oh mercy goodness," said Grandma.

"Honey, I don't know if Danny wants to hear the accordion right now," said Mom, hugging the sleepy baby closer to her. "Maybe later, when he's more awake."

Dad cleared his throat. "Yah," he said, and nodded toward the accordion case. I looked up at him, at his blue eyes that were twinkling now, crinkled in a smile. He liked my accordion playing, always had. And maybe he hadn't carried me in his arms like he did the babies. Maybe my eyes weren't blue. But he was proud I could play that accordion. Proud I was his daughter, too. I could feel it. "Go ahead and play your song for Danny," he said. "He'll like it."

I creaked open my accordion case and touched the cold metal that spoke my name: *Janie Pearson.*

I would play my song for the baby with the dimple in his chin.

~

In just a few days, electricity would be at the farm. My mother had written a poem about it called, "Those Electric Wires of the R.E.A," and it was published in the newspaper. All the intoxicating promises of electricity were embraced in the poem, and hung out for everyone to see. People stopped her on the streets of Conrad, and said they read her poem. Especially farm people who understood it best, and said they didn't know she could write poems like that.

I didn't know if my mother was happier about electricity or the poem, but I supposed it was the electricity, after all. She invited the neighbors over for coffee on the Friday night after the poem was published. "I should have done this before Danny was born," she said to me in the kitchen. "But some of them haven't seen the baby yet, and they want to." They had gone to the Moore's for coffee a while back, and the time before that, to the Rogers'. It really was my mother's turn, but she had never done it before. "Might as well celebrate the lights," she said.

Mom had made a spice cake and the smell of fresh coffee filled the whole house. The Moores came with Margaret, the Rogers with Sonny and Joan. Bernhard and Ole were there, and Emma and Lester Fredrickson with little Donna Kay. Grandma did not come from town for this, because it was too much company, more than she could possibly bear. "All this ruckus, just because they're getting' electricity." I could almost hear her say it.

The adults had the gas lantern in the kitchen, its hissing light illuminating every corner. I wished for one like that, because you could actually read by it. But, as usual, the kids were given a kerosene lamp and we carried it carefully to the bedroom where its glow made everyone's eyes look dark and hooded.

We played dominoes until Sonny got bored, then Old Maid and Authors. Monopoly lay close at hand, should the evening grow longer. In between, Joan told us stories, ghost stories, about a voice quavering from the swamp. "*It flo-o-oats.*" Just before it got too spooky it turned out to be Ivory Soap, and Joan laughed at our scared faces.

"Just a few more days of this," I heard a man's voice say, as he dragged in another chair past us to the kitchen. "By this time next week we'll all have electric lights."

"Can't *wait!*" The women in the kitchen were excited, I could tell by their voices.

Joan heard it, too, and the ghost stories were forgotten. "Just think, we can switch on a light, like they do in town, and we won't have to play games where we can hardly see."

Margaret clapped her hands. Everyone was happy. I knew about lights that switched on. The farm was that much more fun because it didn't have them. The kerosene lamps were fine. I heard Erna Rogers' voice from the kitchen. "I'm getting rid of my old stove, and getting an iron that doesn't have to heat on the top of it. Just plug the iron in the wall and iron your clothes." Murmurs of agreement.

"How 'bout an electric phonograph so you don't have to keep winding your arm off?" It was Ole. He liked music, especially country western. Most likely Bernhard would see that he got an electric phonograph right away.

But it was my mother's voice that sounded the most hopeful of all, eager and full of smiles that I couldn't see. "An electric wash machine," she said. "That's what I want. One I can keep in the house and wash diapers every day." At this, everyone laughed, because they knew all about the babies and the diapers. "And how about those inside bathrooms?"

A cheer burst out in the room, but I turned back to my friends, and the quavering light of the kerosene lamp, the shadows lapping around their faces. Things were changing, all right. Pretty soon the farm would be just like Great Falls, light bulbs and all. And something special would be lost. But I was the only one who thought it, and no one in this farmhouse would agree. Not one.

The flow of voices in the kitchen ebbed away, and someone said it was time to go. It was past Donna Kay's bedtime, in fact, way past. I wanted them to stay longer, but there would be another night like this, even with electricity—a night holding us all close while the frogs croaked down by the barn, and my mother, Harriet, served spice cake and poured fresh coffee into worn cups. More tender nights like this. And days, too. All woven securely into this place where I belong.

The Pearson family having a picnic in the trees behind the farmhouse, summer 1953 from left to right: Jayne; Harriet; Gunder; Grandma Olson; Danny (seated); Nancy; Johnny; Judy; Kitty (in buggy). Not shown: Joe, born 1958